Courtney stood on the deck and watched the wake of the boat disappear in the distance

She and Neil were from two different worlds, and she ought to have the sense to realize it. Sighing, she turned to go into the houseboat.

"I'm back." A haunting emptiness echoed her words.

She stiffened as an undefined apprehension assaulted her from the dark gloom of the houseboat. Something was wrong. Her heart was suddenly pounding as she bounded to her sleeping compartment to check on her baby.

She froze in the doorway when she saw that the bassinet was empty and the diaper bag was gone. She spun on her heels. She searched everywhere…but found nothing, no one.

There was no sign of her baby on the floating house….

Dear Harlequin Intrigue Reader,

This month you'll want to have all six of our books to keep you company as you brave those April showers!

- Debra Webb kicks off THE ENFORCERS, her exciting new trilogy, with *John Doe on Her Doorstep*. And for all of you who have been waiting with bated breath for the newest installment in Kelsey Roberts's THE LANDRY BROTHERS series, we have *Chasing Secrets*.

- Rebecca York, Ann Voss Peterson and Patricia Rosemoor join together in *Desert Sons*. You won't want to miss this unique three-in-one collection!

- Two of your favorite promotions are back. You won't be able to resist Leona Karr's ECLIPSE title, *Shadows on the Lake*. And you'll be on the edge of your seat while reading Jean Barrett's *Paternity Unknown*, the latest installment in TOP SECRET BABIES.

- Meet another of THE PRECINCT's rugged lawmen in Julie Miller's *Police Business*.

Every month you can depend on Harlequin Intrigue to deliver an array of thrilling romantic suspense and mystery. Be sure you read each one!

Sincerely,

Denise O'Sullivan
Senior Editor
Harlequin Intrigue

SHADOWS ON THE LAKE

LEONA KARR

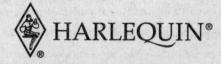

TORONTO • NEW YORK • LONDON
AMSTERDAM • PARIS • SYDNEY • HAMBURG
STOCKHOLM • ATHENS • TOKYO • MILAN • MADRID
PRAGUE • WARSAW • BUDAPEST • AUCKLAND

ISBN 0-373-22840-6

SHADOWS ON THE LAKE

Copyright © 2005 by Leona Karr

www.eHarlequin.com

Printed in U.S.A.

ABOUT THE AUTHOR

A native of Colorado, Leona (Lee) Karr is the author of nearly forty books. Her favorite genres are romantic suspense and inspirational romance. After graduating from the University of Colorado with a B.A. and the University of Northern Colorado with an M.A., she taught as a reading specialist until her first book was published in 1980. She has been on the Waldenbooks bestseller list and nominated by *Romantic Times* for Best Romantic Saga and Best Gothic Author. She has been honored as the Rocky Mountain Fiction Writer of the Year, and received Colorado's Romance Writer of the Year Award. Her books have been reprinted in more than a dozen foreign countries. She is a presenter at numerous writing conferences and has taught college courses in creative writing.

Books by Leona Karr

HARLEQUIN INTRIGUE
120—TREASURE HUNT
144—FALCON'S CRY
184—HIDDEN SERPENT
227—FLASHPOINT
262—CUPID'S DAGGER
309—BODYGUARD
366—THE CHARMER
459—FOLLOW ME HOME
487—MYSTERY DAD
574—INNOCENT WITNESS
623—THE MYSTERIOUS TWIN
672—LOST IDENTITY
724—SEMIAUTOMATIC MARRIAGE
792—A DANGEROUS INHERITANCE
840—SHADOWS ON THE LAKE

LOVE INSPIRED
131—ROCKY MOUNTAIN
    MIRACLE
171—HERO IN DISGUISE
194—HIDDEN BLESSING

CAST OF CHARACTERS

Courtney Collins—A single mother who is the victim of a dangerous deception. What is the fate of her baby boy?

Neil Ellsworth—Drawn into a tangled mesh of love and danger, Neil has secrets of his own. Can the single mother whose baby is missing break down the walls of his hardened heart?

Devanna Davenport—Courtney's aunt has agreed to help her niece under false pretenses. What is the truth hidden in the darkest depths of her personality?

Detective McGrady—This dedicated sleuth with a big heart tracks a murderous kidnapper.

Jake Delaney—An angry business associate who threatens revenge. But will he have to pay the ultimate price in the end?

Steve Woodward—What will happen when the police discover his participation in investment fraud?

Harold Jensen—This kind gentleman had no idea that his past acquaintance with Devanna would forever seal his fate.

Prologue

Dark waters of a mountain lake quietly rippled as a lone woman eased the rowboat to a small dock beside a floating houseboat. After quickly tying up the boat, she made sure there was no sign of the passenger she had left behind in the middle of the lake. It was done, she thought with satisfaction, quietly laughing to herself. She really did have a talent for this sort of thing. Buzz would be proud of her.

From the beginning she'd followed his instructions. She'd made friends with a middle-aged woman, Devanna Davenport, who had rented a houseboat on Lake Manitou, Idaho, and invited her niece and baby to join her for the summer. Fortunately, all arrangements had been made by telephone, and her offer to help Devanna get settled had been accepted. They had arrived at the houseboat that afternoon. As she moved away from the rowboat, a short, otherworldly chuckle escaped her lips.

Inside the houseboat, she unlocked a small locker, and placed her handgun inside. Then she took out a picture of a rugged, stern-looking man wearing a cowboy hat and western clothes. As she held the photo only a few inches from her face, she could feel his breath and read the message in his dark, hypnotic eyes. She had borne the guilt of their aborted bank robbery when he had been shot to death. But Buzz was still with her, still in charge. Willingly, she continued to do his bidding. As his silent voice had instructed, she had arranged to get her hands on a baby boy, and had also found a place to hide until Buzz ordered her to kill and rob again.

"Our son will be here soon," she promised him.

Chapter One

"We're almost there, Jamie," Courtney said as she turned her small car into the parking lot of a café on the outskirts of the bustling resort town of Manitou, Idaho. She smiled back at her four-month-old son as he opened his deep blue eyes. He'd been changed and fed at their last stop, and had been sleeping peacefully in his carrier until the motion of the car stopped.

"I need to stretch my legs, look at a map, and we'll be on our way," she chatted as she got out of the car then reached into the back seat to unfasten his carrier. Being a mother did wonders for developing muscles, she mused as she slung her purse over one shoulder, a diaper bag over the other one, and lifted the baby carrier out of the car. "Here we go, fellow. This is our last stop before we get home."

Home? The word had a mocking sound to it, and Courtney quickly shoved it away. A few weeks' visit with an aunt she hadn't seen since childhood was not a homecoming. During the long drive from Cheyenne, Wyoming, she had begun to question her decision to accept Aunt Devanna's invitation to join her in Manitou where she was renting a houseboat for the summer.

Courtney's husband, Clyde, had been killed in a construction accident a few months before the baby's birth. Except for Aunt Devanna, there were no other members of Courtney's family to quell her loneliness. That's what comes from being an only child, she'd often thought. Her parents had always been on the move because of her father's uncertain employment, and she'd lost both of them before she was twenty-one. She'd put herself through business college, and had married a strong Irishman more out of loneliness than deep love. The union with Clyde Collins had not been one made in heaven.

"You're just tired. Everything will look different when you get some rest," she said, silently encouraging herself as she crossed the parking lot. She felt a decade older than her twenty-nine years, and more alone than ever before.

She'd planned on arriving before dark but night shadows had already spread across the mountain valley, and they were still about five miles from Lake Manitou. She needed to look at her map of the area to locate Hidden Cove, where the houseboat was anchored.

Bright lights and the bustle of the café welcomed her, and some of the tension that had been building in her neck and arms eased as she quickly made her way to the restroom. She blessed the infant changing table as she changed Jamie's diaper. He happily giggled as she playfully buried her face in his tummy and told him what a good boy he was.

After a quick look in the mirror, she combed her straight shoulder-length fair hair and washed her face. She might have brushed on some lipstick, but had no idea where to find it in her bulging purse.

Refreshed, she found an empty booth, set the baby's carrier on the seat, and slipped in beside him. There was a homey feeling about the place, and it seemed popular. Almost all the tables and booths were filled, and Courtney was surprised when a middle-aged waitress came over quickly to take her order.

"What a darling baby," she cooed. "Look at those beautiful blue eyes." Jamie rewarded her flattering attention with a wide, toothless smile.

"His name is Jamie. He's four months," Courtney offered, unable to keep pride out of her voice.

"I have a granddaughter about that age. They're such a blessing, aren't they?" She handed Courtney a menu. "Take a look, and then I'll catch your order."

"Oh, I'll just have coffee, and a ham-and-cheese sandwich."

"We have a special on a four-ounce steak?"

Courtney shook her head. "Just the sandwich."

The steak sounded wonderful, and her taste buds began to quiver at the thought, but she'd kept expenses down during the trip by eating light, and avoiding expensive restaurants and motels.

The accidental life-insurance policy the construction company held on all their workers had paid off at Clyde's death, and if she watched her spending, the money would give her a breathing spell before she had to find some employment.

While she waited for her order, she pulled out a map of the area and spread it on the table. Before she could look at it, Jamie decided he'd had enough of his carrier. His little arms and legs shot out indignantly, and he began to raise a fuss.

"All right, sweetie." Courtney quickly put him on her lap. It wasn't time for him to eat again, so she tried to placate him with his water bottle.

Jamie took the nipple, sucked on it a couple of times, and then spit it out. In one wild sweep of his determined little chubby arms, he sent the water bottle and map careening to the floor.

A man sitting at a nearby table was instantly on his feet. He rescued the map and bottle, smiled at Courtney and chuckled, "I think the little fellow has a mind of his own."

"Thank you," Courtney said quickly, a little embarrassed. The stranger was good-looking, somewhere in his thirties, she guessed. Impeccably dressed, he wore a summer jacket over a soft, open-collar shirt, and tailored deep brown slacks. She decided he had the polished appearance of a businessman. "I'm sorry to have bothered you."

"No problem," he laughingly assured her. "Picking up things is a natural reflex from having more than a dozen nieces and nephews." He chuckled. "They keep their uncle Neil hopping, all right."

NEIL WAS SURPRISED when the attractive woman didn't pick up on the conversational lead he'd given her. Her smile was polite, but nothing more. Usually his most benign comment would spark some interest in the opposite sex, and a friendly conversation would easily follow. She was quite pretty with soft amber hair, arresting blue eyes and a shapely, firm mouth. He had noticed that she wasn't wearing a wedding ring, and his ego smarted just a little. He rose to the challenge.

"I guess you're not from the area," he said indicating the map. "I've lived here most of my life. Maybe I can be of help?"

She shifted the baby from one shoulder to the other, and hesitated a moment before she told him, "I'm joining my aunt for the summer. I was looking for Hidden Cove."

"It's right here." He quickly pointed out the location on the map. Pulling a pencil out of his jacket and bending over the map, he marked it.

"Thank you," she said in that same polite, dismissing tone.

Neil refrained from telling her that Hidden Cove was on the same side of the lake as his home. Her distant and guarded manner didn't invite any casual chitchat. He returned to his table without introducing himself.

BY THE TIME THE WAITRESS brought Courtney's order, the baby had settled down with his pacifier. As she quickly ate her sandwich, she sent several secret glances in the stranger's direction. Shiny, dark wavy hair drifted nicely down on his forehead, and accented dark brown eyes under well-defined brows.

His features were strong and well molded. She noticed that several people stopped at "Uncle Neil's" table to chat with him. From their friendly banter, Courtney concluded he must be well known in the community.

She sighed. As usual she'd handled the situation all wrong. Striking up conversations with strangers had never been easy for her, especially with a man as good-looking as this one. Because her parents had always been on the move, her childhood had been filled with constant warnings about not taking up with people she didn't know. Unfortunately, she'd carried that admonition into adulthood. As a young adult, she'd never been part of a social group, nor had the chance to develop skills that would have allowed her to pursue an acquaintance with an attractive man who had come to her rescue.

Oh, well, she consoled herself. She'd never see him again, and she wouldn't have known what to talk to him about anyway. She kept her eyes away from his table as she paid her bill and walked out of the restaurant.

Neil watched her leave, and wished he'd pointed out the road that would take her around the north side of the lake. If she missed the junction, she could wander around for hours on the wrong side, looking for Hidden Cove.

Impulsively, he quickly took care of his tab, and followed her outside, but as he watched her fasten the baby carrier in the car, he hesitated to approach her. She might misinterpret his helpfulness, and he certainly didn't want to create any kind of a scene. He decided it might be better to get into his own car, and keep a discreet distance behind her as she took the interstate through the center of town. That way, he'd be ready to catch up with her if she missed the correct turnoff.

The prosperous resort town of Manitou hugged the north side of the expansive lake, and frontage roads circled the water on both sides. In his new two-door sports car, it was easy for Neil to keep her taillights in view. When she made the correct turn at the junction, he was pleased.

Most of the women who had passed through his life were totally predictable. No surprises. No challenges. He hadn't met anyone in a long time who intrigued him. Something about the way the young mother had handled herself gave him the impression that she was an interesting combination of softness and honed steel. He couldn't believe he'd let her get away without finding out her name. If she wasn't married, he'd like to know her better. He wondered which one of his neighbors the attractive young mother was going to visit.

His home was one of the scattered, fashionable houses built on the wooded slopes overlooking Hidden Cove. The northern lake road ran between the water's edge on one side, and steep mountain hillsides on the other. He was puzzled when she began to slow down because all the homes in the cove were still some distance ahead. He stiffened. Was something wrong with her car? Did she have a flat tire?

She kept going at a slow speed as if looking for something. When she pulled into a narrow parking area above the lake, he let out a soft whistle. So that's where she was headed! Her destination must be one of the houseboats nestled around the cove.

Well, what do you know? he thought. His real estate company handled the rentals on those particular houseboats. As he headed up the steep winding road to his home, he laughed softly. He was pretty sure he could come up with a good reason to drop by and check on his renters.

Courtney found a parking space marked with the number her aunt had written her. She sat in the car for a long minute before getting out. A brisk wind had come up and she could see ruffled water on the dark lake catching glimmers of moonlight as ripples moved restlessly upon the shore. The scene was a foreign one to her. Because she'd never been around the water very much, she'd never learned to swim. Living in a floating house would be a new experience for her, and she wasn't sure she'd like it all that much. A strange sense of dread settled on her as she sat there and struggled with some undefined reluctance to get out of the car.

"I'm just tired," she said aloud. "Come on, honey bun. Let's go meet your auntie."

Holding the baby securely, she descended narrow steps leading to a narrow dock and the houseboat snugged up to it. She'd unpack the car later when she had Jamie settled. She had brought only necessities with her and had stored her few possessions for the summer.

An orangish light mounted on a high pole above the stairs gave an eerie cast to the brown, boxlike structure. The name of the houseboat, *Nevermore,* was carved in a wooden sign swinging in the wind, and a small rowboat tethered at the small dock made a moaning, sucking sound.

A sliver of light edged one of the curtained windows and was the only sign of occupancy. Courtney knew Aunt Devanna had only taken possession of the houseboat a few days ago, but she'd written that she had hired a woman to help her get settled.

A relentless flickering of shadows on the surrounding lake, and the play of boards under Courtney's feet, added to her growing uneasiness as she stepped on the narrow deck of the houseboat and approached the front door.

Shifting the baby, she freed one arm and knocked loudly on the weathered wood. Nothing happened. Not a sound from inside.

She knocked again and the door opened slightly. She sensed someone peeking out, but couldn't clearly see who it was. Courtney knew her aunt hadn't seen her since she was a youngster, and they'd never exchanged photographs, so she quickly identified herself.

"It's me, Aunt Devanna. I'm sorry to be arriving so late. You gave good directions in your letter," she offered the reassurance. "I found the houseboat without any trouble."

The door slowly opened and a woman was silhouetted by the small light behind her. Courtney couldn't see her features clearly as she opened the door wider and motioned her inside.

When she didn't say anything, Courtney said, "I

really appreciate your invitation to come and spend the summer with you."

As they stepped into the light, Courtney could see that her aunt was a rather plain, sturdy woman, about five foot eleven, with hair obviously dyed to cover any gray. She was plainly dressed in slacks and a pullover, and looked a lot younger and healthier than Courtney had expected.

The frown on her aunt's face eased as her gaze dropped to the baby in Courtney's arms, and a visible warmth rose in her face.

"This is Jamie," Courtney said quickly, pleased at her aunt's reaction. As she reached for the baby, Courtney promptly handed Jamie into her waiting arms. "He's probably ready for his nightly bottle and another diaper change."

"A baby boy." Her aunt's voice was soft and loving as she gazed at the infant. "How old?"

"Four months," Courtney answered. Her aunt must have forgotten that she'd told her his age in one of her letters. At the time, Courtney had been concerned that Devanna wouldn't appreciate all the fuss and paraphernalia that a baby required, but that worry was put to rest as she watched her aunt sit on the couch, cuddling Jamie.

How sad that Devanna had never had any children of her own, Courtney thought, watching her with the baby. Her aunt had married a man twice her age, and when he died, she'd inherited a modest lifetime income that allowed her to withdraw into herself and live as a recluse. She must be close to fifty years old now.

Courtney's mother had rarely heard from her sister. Apparently there had been some friction between them. After her mother's death, an exchange of Christmas cards with her aunt had been the extent of their communication until Devanna learned of the death of Courtney's husband and the birth of the baby. No one was more surprised than Courtney when her aunt made the effort to mend family ties. As Courtney watched Devanna with the baby, she was glad she'd decided to come.

Glancing around the houseboat, Courtney could see her aunt had made little, if any, preparation for their arrival. In fact, it didn't even look as if Devanna had gotten herself settled in. A galleylike kitchen area at one side of the room had numerous boxes sitting on the counters. There were stacks of books on the floor waiting to be put on shelves. Clothes were piled on chairs in the sitting and dining areas.

"Haven't had time to straighten up," her aunt said as she watched Courtney's gaze pass over the clutter.

"I thought you had hired a woman to help you."

"She didn't work out," she answered flatly. "I had to get rid of her." For an instant it seemed as if a faint smile hovered on her lips.

"Oh, that's too bad," Courtney answered, puzzled why her aunt would be pleased about the situation. "Well, I'm here now, and you can tell me what needs to be done."

Jamie let out a wail that settled matters for the moment. Courtney hurriedly heated a bottle and accepted her aunt's offer to give it to him.

"Thanks, I'll go bring everything in from the car. I need to boil some bottles and water for a new batch of formula."

"You'll teach me how," her aunt ordered in a commanding tone that startled Courtney. "You'll show me everything."

"Yes, of course," she responded, totally surprised, not knowing exactly how to handle her aunt's insistence on caring for the baby.

Courtney made several trips up and down the narrow steps as she unloaded the car. The houseboat was a big disappointment. All imaginary pleasures of living on the water quickly faded as Courtney realized what little privacy she was going to have.

Having seen Hollywood's version of romantic life aboard such accommodations, Courtney had allowed herself a foolish hope that her visit would be, at the very least, a change from her humdrum routine. The present situation mocked those idle fantasies.

There was more living space in some of the modern RVs Courtney had seen. The houseboat sitting area was divided from a small galley by a counter and barstools. The kitchen included a three-burner cooktop and a small refrigerator crowded with just the things Courtney had unloaded from the ice chest. No dishwasher, but it was blessed with a compact clothes dryer mounted on top of a washing machine. At least she wouldn't have go out every day to wash the baby's soiled clothes.

There were two sleeping quarters, small but private.

"That's mine," her aunt said in a warning tone to

Courtney and she quickly shut the door of one, as if to emphasize that it was off-limits. "You and the baby take that one," she said curtly, pointing to a door opposite hers.

The sleeping compartment was postage-stamp sized with bunk beds, a small closet, and barely enough floor space to turn around. Courtney set Jamie's bassinet on the lower bunk, settled him in it, and eyed the top bed with less than enthusiasm.

"It's plenty big," her aunt said in an argumentative tone when Courtney didn't say anything.

"And the bathroom?"

"Right there." Devanna pointed out a minuscule bathroom crammed in between the two sleeping compartments. The floor space was scarcely big enough for the necessities of toilet and shower, and a couple of small shelves were already filled with her aunt's toiletries.

Courtney's expression must have registered her irritation because her aunt quickly opened the door of a small cupboard under the sink. "You can put your stuff here. And there are some extra towels for the baby—and you."

Devanna smiled with such satisfaction that Courtney was taken aback by the sudden warmth in her eyes. Maybe everything was going to work out after all.

"I'll get Jamie bedded down for the night, and then we can talk." Courtney said, anxious to keep her aunt in a good mood. Even though she was dead tired, she knew it was important that they get off to a good start.

Her aunt's behavior was not at all what Courtney had expected from her friendly letter. Except for her loving attention to the baby, Devanna seemed totally indifferent to Courtney's presence. Her responses to questions were vague and noncommittal. Even though Courtney knew her aunt had been a recluse most of her life, her lack of social skills was startling.

As soon as Jamie nodded off to sleep, Courtney returned to the sitting room to have some quiet time with her aunt, but she wasn't there and her sleeping compartment door was closed.

Courtney made a cup of tea, hoping it would help her stay awake until her aunt returned and they could chat. She eased down in a recliner chair that was as well worn as the couch.

The dank, musty smell that Courtney had noticed before seemed even stronger as she sat there in the muted light. The constant sound of a mooring chain clanking against the dock scraped her nerves. As the wind battering the houseboat grew stronger, the ever-present movement of the floors increased under her feet. A sharp peppering of rain against the black windows created a trapped feeling that finally brought her to her feet.

She'd waited long enough. The get-acquainted conversation with her aunt would have to wait until tomorrow. Jamie was sleeping peacefully as she kissed his warm cheek. Just looking at him, she had a sense of purpose in her life that she'd never had before.

As she settled in the upper bunk, a cacophony of weird noises echoed across the water. They were like voices rising and falling in warning. Courtney tried to close her ears to them. Tomorrow in the sunshine, everything would feel different.

Wouldn't it?

Chapter Two

Courtney spent a restless night, and it seemed to her she'd just dropped off to sleep when Jamie made his presence known and demanded his early-morning bottle. She threw on a robe and picked him up.

His demanding cries would surely wake her aunt at this ungodly hour, she thought as she tried to hush him, but as she hurried past Devanna's closed door, muted sounds of someone talking and laughing were faintly audible.

Did she have someone in the room with her? The idea was so preposterous, Courtney quickly shoved it away. A radio! Of course. Devanna must be an early riser, listening to an early wake-up program, Courtney decided as she hurried to the kitchen.

Having some company at this early-breakfast hour would be a pleasant change, Courtney thought as she laid the baby on the sofa, changed his diaper, and braced him with pillows while she heated his bottle. She expected her aunt to join them at any time, but Jamie finished his bottle and dropped off to sleep, and still Devanna hadn't come out of her room.

As Courtney passed the closed door on her way to put Jamie in his bassinet, she listened for the earlier sounds, but there was only silence. Apparently her aunt had fallen back asleep.

Courtney eyed the top bunk, but decided to get dressed instead of going back to bed. She debated about taking a shower before she dressed for the day. If Devanna had gone back to sleep, she didn't want the sound of the water to awaken her. Better wait until later, after they'd established some kind of mutual routine, she decided.

A displaced feeling was steadily growing in spite of the fact she'd only just arrived. It was probably fatigue that was making her feel jumpy, she reasoned as put on her last pair of clean jeans and a comfortable summer knit top. She'd quickly lost the weight she'd gained with Jamie, and her wardrobe was very pragmatic, mostly denims and summer cottons. She doubted that she'd need anything more during her visit. Her one good outfit would do if Devanna wanted to go out somewhere.

The rain had stopped during the night, leaving a moist fog behind. As the sun began to break through lingering gray clouds, wispy tendrils of a mist rose from the lake. As Courtney looked out the windows, she felt as if the houseboat were floating away into an unknown dimension of nothingness.

It was midmorning before Devanna emerged from her room. She wore dark slacks and a plain green blouse. In the daylight, her complexion looked ruddy, and the deep creases in her forehead showed.

"I made coffee," Courtney told her quickly, wanting to get the day started off right. "And I could fix you something."

"I don't eat breakfast," she answered ungraciously. "Where's the baby?"

"Asleep, but he should be waking up anytime now. I'll be giving him his bath." Courtney smiled. "He likes it. Splashes water all over the place."

Devanna just gave a dismissing wave of her hand. "I've got business this morning."

Clearly, her aunt had other things on her mind as she walked over to the counter and picked up a notepad. "Here's the grocery order. The delivery boy will pick it up when he makes today's delivery. Make a list of what you want, and he'll bring it next time."

"We don't have a phone?"

"Not unless you're to fork up the deposit and pay the monthly charges. Not worth the money to me." She added, "Paying the city for electricity and water hookups isn't cheap, either."

"I'll pay my share of everything."

"Then I think we'll get along."

After she left, Courtney realized that her aunt hadn't left any money on the counter for the grocery order. When the boy came, she paid for the delivery and gave him both grocery lists.

"Thanks," he said when she gave him a tip, and looked surprised, as if he hadn't expected one.

Her aunt was gone for most of the day. A poignant loneliness mocked Courtney's high hopes for the summer. How she had looked forward to enjoying a sense of "family," instead of facing the world on her own! When Aunt Devanna had reached out to her, she felt that she wasn't totally alone anymore, but nothing could have been further from the feelings that plagued her now.

Ever since she'd arrived, her aunt's welcome would have been totally without any interest or warmth except for the baby. Why? What had happened? Was Devanna regretting the invitation she'd extended in her letter?

As the hours crept by, Courtney struggled to understand her aunt's behavior. Living as a recluse for years had made her aunt a loner. No doubt about it.

I'll just have to be patient, she told herself, entertaining a pang of sympathy for her aunt. I'll win her over. Instead of judging her, I'll find ways to make her life a little happier, and, hopefully, change some of her eccentric behavior.

DESPITE COURTNEY'S valiant efforts, several days passed without much change in her aunt's behavior. Her disinterest in Courtney continued, at the same time her growing devotion to the baby intensified. Devanna quickly learned Jamie's schedule, and was eager to feed him, change his diaper and lull him to sleep.

Courtney couldn't have found a better nursemaid. With time on her hands, getting the houseboat in shape fell to Courtney. She organized her aunt's belongings as best she could, and was puzzled at Devanna's disinterest in the books she'd brought, and the unfinished embroidery in her sewing basket.

When Devanna wasn't caring for the baby, she spent a lot of time in her room with the door shut.

Other times, she left the houseboat in her gray van without offering any explanations as to where she was going, or where she'd gone. She had a habit of bringing back fast food for herself, but never any for Courtney.

"I didn't know what you'd like."

Why didn't you ask? Her aunt's lack of interest in any open communication between them baffled Courtney. Devanna never reminisced about the past, nor shared any childhood memories of growing up with Courtney's mother. Any attempt to engage her in casual conversation fell flat.

Even though they were docked, Courtney felt isolated from everything and everyone by water, so she spent uninterrupted hours on the narrow deck encircling the houseboat. The weather had turned clear and warm, and the view of the surrounding mountains and the ever-changing water of the lake was a balm to her growing discomfort.

She loved watching the activity on the lake. Private boats, large and small, dotted the dark blue waters. Water-skiers created white wakes like rooster tails as they skimmed by, and two commercial tourist vessels made many runs a day. Sandy beaches were filled with swimmers of all ages, but Courtney never had the urge to get into the water herself.

She spent time reading some of her aunt's books, but when she spied a small ladder leading to the flat roof of the houseboat, she welcomed a new way to spend her idle time. A perfect place for sunbathing!

Her spirits rose as she quickly changed into her

swimsuit and grabbed her suntan lotion. Since her aunt had disappeared on one of her mysterious drives, and Jamie was taking a morning nap, she was free to have a pleasant time in the sun.

She climbed up the ladder, and was getting ready to stretch out on the roof when the noise of an approaching boat caught her attention. A sleek cruiser skimmed the water with a foamy wake, and she watched as it docked at another houseboat a short distance away.

Her sigh was filled with envy. The old rowboat that her aunt had said came with the rental of their houseboat didn't appeal to her, and she doubted that she would ever try to take it out on the lake.

Keeping a motherly ear for any sound of Jamie, Courtney let herself relax for the first time since her arrival. The warm sun felt lovely. After a few minutes, she sat up, preparing to turn over on her back, but as she glanced across the water, she was startled to see the sleek cruiser heading in her direction.

As it came closer, she could see a man wearing a nautical cap and white sports clothes at the wheel. She couldn't believe it when he eased the boat into their dock, next to the rowboat.

Who in the world?

Hurriedly, she descended the ladder and made her way around the deck to the dock side. She was absolutely stunned when she came face-to-face with the man she'd encountered at the restaurant the night of her arrival. She couldn't find her voice to even say hello.

Neil pretended to be as totally surprised to see her.

"Well, I'll be! Can you believe it? Remember me? The rescuer of baby bottles and maps?"

More than once the helpful stranger had been in Courtney's thoughts as she'd wondered what would have happened if she'd only seized the opportunity to get to know him.

He laughed deeply at her astonishment and held out his hand. "Neil Ellsworth. It's nice to see you again. I guess it's a small world, after all."

"Yes it is," she echoed. "Courtney Collins."

Her hand felt soft, yet firm in his. "Nice to meet you, Courtney."

"Why—?" she stammered. "I mean I don't understand. What brought you here?"

"Business," he answered with a solemnity that contrasted with the twinkle in his eye and the curve of his lips.

She smiled back. "What kind of business?"

"I'm your landlord."

"What?" she gasped in total surprise. "You own this houseboat?"

Chuckling, he shook his head. "No, but my company handles the rental on most of the houseboats in Hidden Cove."

"You've got to be kidding."

"It's true." He launched into the explanation he'd mentally prepared. "Since all the arrangements for *Nevermore* were made by mail, I thought I'd introduce myself to Devanna Davenport and see if the accommodations were satisfactory. She must be the aunt you told me you were joining for the summer. What a coincidence."

"I'm afraid she isn't here right now."

"Oh, that's too bad. I didn't see a phone listing or I would have called ahead."

"If you'd like to wait…?" She felt heat rising in her cheeks as she suddenly realized she was standing there in a very brief, hot-pink swimming suit that had never touched water. She'd bought it at a secondhand store, just for sunbathing.

"Thanks, I think I will. If it's no trouble?"

"I was enjoying the sun, but I've really had enough for the first time out," she lied. "Would you like to come inside? I think there's some lemonade in the fridge."

"Sounds great."

As Neil followed her inside, he mentally patted himself on the back for orchestrating a way to see her again. Her slender figure was perfection in the revealing two-piece bathing suit, and the way she moved was sexy enough to stimulate his masculine desires. The pleasure of cupping her enticing backside with his caressing hands crossed his mind as she walked in front of him. She was every bit as physically attractive as he had remembered, but there was something more that had captured his interest from the beginning.

Ever since their casual meeting, he'd been asking himself what it was about her that intrigued him. Maybe it was a kind of melancholy vulnerability, or a challenging independence that reminded him of a frightened child bowing her neck to fight the world. Whatever the attraction, he only knew she touched some responsive chord deep within him, and he was drawn to her in some undefined way.

"Excuse me for a minute," she said apologetically. "I need to check on Jamie. I'll just be a minute."

"No problem." He sat down on one of the counter barstools to wait.

As Neil glanced around the clean and tidy room, he was satisfied he could reassure the owner that Devanna Davenport was a satisfactory renter. He was anxious to meet the aunt. Was she anything like her niece? he wondered.

When Courtney returned a few minutes later, he saw she'd draped a saronglike garment over her swimming suit. As far as Neil was concerned, the soft, clinging material only heightened the tantalizing lines and curves of her figure. He indulged in a fleeting masculine fantasy of drawing her close and feeling her loveliness pressed against him. Regretfully, he forced his thoughts back to reality and inquired politely about the baby.

"He's still asleep," she said, smiling. "He's settled into the change nicely."

"And what about you? Is living on the water to your liking?" Something in her bright tone seemed slightly false.

"I'm not sure." Faint worry lines marred the smoothness of her brow.

"It may take some getting used to," he offered.

"I guess so."

Something in the situation was weighing heavily on her, Neil was sure of it. Even though he knew he should distance himself from any concerns about her private life, he couldn't. The fact that he'd gone to such lengths to see her again mocked any indifference to her welfare.

"I hope this is sweet enough for you," she said as she set down a pitcher and two glasses, and then took a stool beside him.

He took a sip. "Perfect."

"You're easy to please," she said, smiling at him.

"Nope, to the contrary. My family accuses me of being the worst perfectionist in the world."

"Tell me about your family," she urged. In her childhood, she'd been the little girl looking through a fence, watching the extended family next door gathered for a family celebration. "I know you have a lot of nieces and nephews." He'd referred to himself as "uncle" at the restaurant.

"I have four brothers and two sisters. They're all great. One sister, and my younger twin brothers live in Manitou."

She listened, captivated, as he talked about a large overflowing family, with deep roots planted in this community where he was raised.

"My parents are retired and enjoy traveling without a parcel of kids underfoot. All of my siblings are married and I'm the only single one left."

"Why is that?"

"Oh, I'm not a good candidate for marriage," he replied lightly, but there was a flickering of shadow in his dark brown eyes, and Courtney wondered what had put it there. "Of course, everyone tells me I haven't met the right woman. What do you think?"

"I don't know," she answered honestly, at a loss when it came to understanding the desires of the heart. "There are a lot of reasons for getting married, I guess."

"And divorced?" he asked pointedly.

She knew what he was asking. "I'm not divorced."

He listened attentively as she told him about the unexpected death of Jamie's father several months before the baby was born. "He was a construction worker. A faulty beam fell six stories, and killed him."

"I'm sorry. How long had you been married?"

"A couple of years."

When she didn't volunteer any more personal information about her marriage, he refrained from asking any more questions. He hated it when people tried to dig around in his past. It wasn't anybody's business why he'd decided to forgo marriage.

They sipped their lemonade in silence until Courtney offered quietly, "I'm trying to get my life back together. I thought spending the summer with my aunt would help, but…" Her voice trailed off.

"Things aren't working out the way you thought?"

She shook her head. "Maybe it's me, but…" She might have said more but they heard the sound of footsteps on the deck.

Her aunt was back.

Neil instantly rose to his feet as Devanna came in. "Mrs. Davenport. How nice to meet you. I'm Neil Ellsworth. I handled your rental through the Ellsworth Real Estate and Investment Company."

"Of course," she responded with only the slightest hesitation. Her eyes lowered just slightly as if her thoughts were racing ahead. "Is there some problem?"

"Oh, not at all," Neil assured her. "Just making a routine check on all the rented houseboats. I want to make sure everything is satisfactory."

"How nice of you." She visibly relaxed and smiled. "We don't have many handsome men calling on us, do we, Courtney?"

"I find that hard to believe," Neil responded gallantly.

Courtney couldn't believe the metamorphosis in her aunt's behavior. She was all smiles and began gushing about how wonderful it was to have her niece and the baby staying with her.

"I'm glad the houseboat is working out for you."

"Oh, it is," she assured him. "Lots of privacy. No nosy neighbors gawking at you. We don't have even one complaint, do we Courtney?"

The ease with which her aunt was able to change her persona so dramatically disturbed Courtney in a way she didn't understand. She was glad when Jamie's protesting wail alerted her and she quickly excused herself.

She left Neil and Devanna chatting pleasantly, and when she returned with the baby a few minutes later, she was surprised to find that Devanna had already heated his bottle.

"Here, let me have him," Devanna ordered. "He likes to have Auntie feed him, don't you, sweetheart?" She took the baby out of Courtney's arms and sat down on the couch to give him his bottle.

"Your aunt tells me you haven't been away from

the houseboat at all, Courtney. I was wondering if you'd like to have lunch with me at the marina?" Neil asked, giving her one of his people-management smiles.

"Oh, I'm afraid I couldn't," Courtney responded quickly. "The baby—"

"Is obviously in good hands," he finished for her. "You really should take some time for yourself."

"I agree," Devanna said firmly. "She's been much too gloomy to be good company."

I haven't been the only one, Courtney wanted to snap back, but restrained herself.

"The baby will be fine. Won't you, darling?" Smiling down at Jamie, Devanna cooed, "Such a sweet, sweet, sweety pie. Auntie loves you."

Courtney's feelings were mixed. Should she leave the baby? Her aunt had taken enough care of him to reassure her that he'd be in good hands. It was true she'd slipped into a funk since her arrival. Getting away for a few hours might put some life back into her. Just thinking about being with other people tempted her to accept the invitation. She had no idea why Neil wanted to bother himself like this, but could she refuse?

"It's settled then," Neil said hopefully.

She nodded. "Give me a few minutes to change."

When she returned, Neil smiled appreciatively at her nicely fitted denim slacks and yellow knit top that brought out the golden highlights in her hair. Her skin was lightly burnished from her time in the sun, and an excited sparkle in her eyes matched the lightness of her step.

She kissed the baby, gave her aunt some instructions about baby food and then turned to him. "I guess I'm ready."

"Would you like to take a spin around the lake before we head for the marina?" he asked her as they settled themselves in his speedboat.

"If you have the time. I don't want to interfere with your work."

"Pleasure before business anytime," he assured her, grinning.

His relaxed good humor was infectious. As the boat skimmed over the water, Courtney became a part of the scene she'd been watching from the deck of the houseboat. She lifted her face boldly to the wind and let her hair fly free. She laughed with Neil when the spray from a nearby boat bathed both of them.

She couldn't believe she was actually going to lunch with such a charming, attractive man. He'd made it clear that he wasn't interested in any serious commitments, and that was fine with her. She'd never felt such freedom to enjoy the moment and put aside any thoughts about the future.

Neil was delighted with her childlike pleasure. She was different from the women he was used to dating. Most of them were concerned about how they looked while they role-played the femme fatale. He was pleased that once Courtney seemed secure enough to lower her guard, there was no pretense about her. He wondered about her background, and was determined to know a lot more about her before their lunch date was over.

As they headed for the far end of the lake, Hidden Cove disappeared behind them and the brown houseboat was lost from view.

AS SHE SAT IN FRONT OF Buzz's photo, her eyes sparkled with happiness. Laughing joyfully, she held up the baby for him to see.

"Look, darling. Just like we always planned. Our very own baby boy. Remember how you promised me a child of my own some day?" She snuggled against Jamie's soft cheek. "And here he is. The moment I laid eyes on him, I knew he was ours."

Her expression sobered as she cocked her head and listened. "Yes, I know, Buzz. But don't worry. I'll make another hit, and then I'll have money to travel. I've been checking out some of the banks."

She listened again, frowning. "It's okay, Buzz. Relax, honey. I have plans to take care of the woman soon."

Cuddling the baby in her arms, she began to hum a lullaby.

NEIL DOCKED THE BOAT at the marina in a recreational area that stretched several blocks along the lake. The beautifully landscaped area was inviting with clean, sandy beaches, winding paths, park benches and nearby colorful shops. With Courtney walking beside him, Neil was surprised how her presence made him view everything with a fresh eye.

She commented on flower beds, fountains and lush green lawns, and when she saw mothers pushing baby carriages and strollers, she exclaimed excitedly, "I'll have to bring Jamie here."

"Maybe you and my sister Maribeth could arrange a play date. She has two little ones."

Courtney gave a vague nod of her head. She thought it wasn't likely that his sister would follow through on the idea.

"You'd like her," he added with a smile. "She's my youngest sister. There's only a couple years difference between us, and I guess I'm closer to her than the others. I can always tell when she's feeling down, and needs a pick-me-up." He grinned at Courtney. "She has eyes that give her feelings away—just like you do."

"I'm that easy to read?"

"Not entirely," he assured her.

"Well, thank you for rescuing me."

"My pleasure. What kind of food do you like?"

"Any kind I don't have to cook," she readily replied. "A hot dog would be just fine."

"Oh, I think I can do better than that." He boldly slipped his arm through hers.

They walked several blocks to a small café in a Victorian house, complete with an old-fashioned cupola and gingerbread trim. A plump hostess dressed in old-fashioned costume greeted Neil with a welcoming smile and gave Courtney a quick assessing glance as if interested in seeing whom he was squiring for lunch.

"A nice table outside?" she asked Neil as if the question were rhetorical. Courtney suspected the hostess was asking if he wanted his usual table.

"What would you like?" he asked, deferring to Courtney. "Inside or out?"

"Outside sounds nice," she readily replied. She'd had enough of being cooped up in a houseboat, eating meals at a counter.

A canopy of trees shaded the wide veranda, and the hostess led them to a table near a fountain spilling water into a small pond circled by feathery green ferns. The faint perfume of roses touched Courtney's nostrils and she drew in the heavenly scent. The fragrance was a sharp contrast to the musty, dank smell of the houseboat.

Neil held Courtney's chair and then took a seat opposite her. The hostess handed them an ornate menu decorated with cupids and flourishes of flowers and birds.

"Thank you, Harriet."

"My pleasure." She gave Neil a knowing smile. "Please enjoy."

Courtney took one look at the prices and knew the Victorian café would never be mistaken for a fast-food establishment.

"See anything you like?" Neil asked, seeing her frown as she studied the elaborate selections.

How could she make a choice when every single entrée stimulated her taste buds? "What do you usually have?"

"Well, let's see." He readily pointed out several selections, confirming that he dined there often.

She didn't know about his usual luncheon dates, but if he expected her to order something dainty like a watercress salad, he was in for a surprise.

After a careful job of elimination, she said, "I think I'll have lentil soup, baked pork with applesauce, creamed asparagus and scalloped potatoes. Raisin bread pudding for dessert." She closed the menu and leaned back in her chair.

"Good choice." He chuckled silently. Her frank appetite appealed to him. It was refreshing to date a woman who enjoyed good food and made no bones about it. "I think I'll have the same. Would you like a drink while we're waiting? I recommend an English beer. It goes great with pork."

His twinkling eyes challenged her, but she shook her head. "I'll settle for a pot of tea, please."

As they waited for their orders, he entertained her with stories about the community and his family. "I took over the Ellsworth Real Estate and Investment Company when my dad decided to call it quits."

"And you like it?"

"Most of the time. I've made some mistakes. Trusted some people I shouldn't have." A shadow flickered in his brown eyes, and Courtney waited for him to explain but he changed the subject.

When their food arrived, conversation petered off into brief comments about the delicious fare. He smiled as she lifted a delicate china teapot and poured the fragrant brew into a gold-rimmed teacup.

"What?"

"Nothing."

"Then why are you smiling?"

"There was such pleasure in your face, I couldn't help picturing you at an elegant tea party, offering gold-rimmed cups to fashionable guests."

She laughed. "Nothing could be further from the truth. I don't think we ever had cups that weren't chipped, and no two alike. Every time we moved, which was often, we had to start from scratch replacing what we'd broken or left behind."

"What did your father do?"

"He was a welder. Not a very good one, I'm afraid," she said sadly. "He tried hard, but never stayed with any job for very long. I put myself through business college, and was working as a secretary for a construction company when I met my husband, Clyde." She paused. "Our marriage had its challenges."

"Well, I decided a long time ago I'm not husband or father material."

Undoubtedly, more than one unattached female considered him a good catch, Courtney thought. She wanted to assure him that she wasn't looking for a man to complicate her life. Even though she had married out of loneliness, there had been very little companionship in her marriage, and the tender love she'd desperately sought had evaded her. She certainly wasn't about to open herself to that kind of heartache again.

She gave her attention to the delicious pudding steeped in brandy sauce, and finished the last bite when she glanced at her watch.

"Oh, my goodness, I've got to get back. Jamie is always fussing after his noontime nap." She instantly felt a sense of guilt for putting her son completely out of her mind for nearly three hours.

"He's in good hands," Neil reassured her. "While you were getting dressed, your aunt told me how much Jamie means to her. I guess she's never had children of her own. Anyone can see she feels very possessive about him."

"I'm beginning to think Jamie is the only reason she invited us to come," Courtney said honestly. "It's been quite a disappointment. I thought she and I would become friends and enjoy a special companionship this summer. But it's not happening."

"You've only been here a few days," he reminded her. "If she's not used to living with anyone, it may take a little time for her to adjust."

"I suppose so."

"You'll win her over."

Courtney wished she could be that optimistic. She couldn't understand her aunt's baffling behavior, let alone find a way to change it. She dreaded returning to the houseboat's oppressive atmosphere and negative energy, but her son was her first priority. She had no business running around, thinking about her own pleasure.

When they docked beside the houseboat, Courtney thanked Neil for the outing.

"Maybe we should do this again," he suggested.

"I don't think I should make a habit of being away from the baby, but thank you for today."

There was a finality in her refusal that surprised him because she'd given him every indication that she had enjoyed his company. Obviously, she wasn't as taken with him as he had been with her, he decided, his pride smarting just a little. He wasn't used to having women turn him down.

"Enjoy your visit," he said in a polite tone. As he waved goodbye from his boat, he didn't think he'd give her a chance to reject him again.

Courtney stood for a moment on the deck and

watched the wake of the boat disappear in the distance. They were from two different worlds, and she ought to have the sense to realize it. Sighing, she turned into the houseboat.

"I'm back."

A haunting emptiness echoed her words.

She stiffened as an undefined apprehension assaulted her from the dark gloom of the houseboat. Something was wrong. She could feel it.

Her heart was suddenly pounding as she bounded to the sleeping compartment to check on her baby.

She froze in the doorway when she saw Jamie's bassinet was empty, and the diaper bag she kept at the front of the lower bunk gone.

She spun on her heels. The only place left was her aunt's compartment. Maybe her aunt had taken him into her sleeping room. Anxiously, she opened the door and looked in.

Empty.

No sign of Jamie or Aunt Devanna anywhere in the floating house.

Chapter Three

Fighting back rising panic, Courtney dashed around the narrow deck to the stern end of the houseboat. Sometimes her aunt spent time sitting there, but her chair was empty and no baby things in sight. The houseboat creaked with emptiness as Courtney checked again, inside and out. Then she took the narrow steps two at a time up to the parking area.

Her aunt's gray van was gone.

Courtney couldn't believe it. Devanna had taken Jamie somewhere! For a moment, anger overrode Courtney's anxiety. She was furious! Her aunt had no business taking the baby anywhere without her permission.

Courtney started for her car and then stopped. *Get hold of yourself!* Common sense mocked her impulse to go chasing after the van. What good would it do, driving around blindly, trying to find them? She hadn't the foggiest idea where her aunt might have gone. *I shouldn't have left my baby,* Courtney mentally lashed herself.

Pacing up and down, she fought to calm a hurricane of fear. It was time for Jamie to have another feeding. Had Devanna taken a bottle with her? How long had they been gone? A few minutes? Or had Devanna driven away with Jamie as soon as Courtney and Neil had been out of sight?

Her eyes kept searching the lake road in both directions, and all types of scenarios filled her mind. There'd been an accident! The van had developed engine trouble! Jamie had gotten sick and Devanna had rushed him to the hospital! There was no telephone in the houseboat. Should she go somewhere to call someone? But who? Every time a car came into view, Courtney's hopes rose, and then quickly fell. She even walked a short distance up and down the road as if that might hurry their return.

When the gray van finally came into view, Courtney thought she might be hallucinating until it slowed and pulled into the parking area.

Letting out a cry of relief, she rushed over to it. Her aunt gave her an innocent smile as she jerked open the front door and settled her frantic gaze on Jamie.

Thank God! The baby was securely fastened in his carrier and sound asleep. His little face was peaceful and content, and Courtney was weak with a combination of relief, frustration and anger.

"He was fussy, so I took him for a little ride. You weren't worried, were you?" Devanna asked. The funny little quirk to her lips might have been a suppressed smile.

"What do you think?" Courtney snapped. "You scared me half to death, taking him off like that."

Devanna looked surprised. "You should have known I'd never let anything happen to Jamie. You don't have to worry when he's with me."

As Courtney took the baby out of the car, he opened his eyes and gave her one of his toothless smiles. She blinked back tears of thankfulness. He was all right. She'd been worried for nothing.

"He's precious, isn't he?" Devanna cooed. "And such a good baby. He settled right down once we were in the car. I brought his diaper bag along just in case."

Her aunt seemed so sincere that Courtney felt guilty about lashing out at her. She should have known that her aunt was responsible when it came to taking care of Jamie. Her love for the baby was undeniable.

"And how was your lunch with that handsome fellow?" Devanna asked when they were back inside the houseboat.

"Very nice," Courtney said honestly.

"I guess he'll be coming around again?"

"I don't think so."

"That's too bad," Devanna answered, thoughtfully. "I thought you'd enjoy getting out, now and again."

Courtney looked at her in surprise. Usually Devanna ignored her unless the situation had something to do with the baby. This was the first time her aunt had expressed any interest in her well-being. Maybe things were going to smooth out between them after all.

Unfortunately, the next few days Devanna seemed

more preoccupied than ever, and in a world of her own. She left the houseboat frequently, and Court-ney continued to hear radiolike talking and laughing in the middle of the night.

Devanna's only consistency was her attention to Jamie. She was ready and willing to take over his care as much as Courtney would allow. The baby provided the only real sharing between the two women. Most of the time, Devanna seemed lost in her own world, and Courtney's hope that a friendly companionship would develop between them quickly died.

A greater sense of loneliness than before settled on Courtney, especially when she thought about Neil. She relived over and over the time they'd spent together. Clearly, he was content with his single life, and a lonely widow wasn't in his future. She'd never been one to lie to herself, and trying to make a Cin-derella story out of their relationship would be pure stupidity. Neil might be interested in a light summer flirtation, but she didn't want to go there. She'd never been able to center her life for momentary pleasures, and now, more than ever, she had to think about the future because of her precious Jamie. Yes, she'd done the right thing turning down his tentative suggestion of another date.

During one of Devanna's absences from the houseboat, Courtney was lounging on the couch, reading one the books her aunt had brought—and never looked at—when there was a knock at the door. Her heartbeat instantly quickened.

Neil! Maybe he'd come back to see her.

Nervously she smoothed her hair, straightening the collar of her summer blouse, and took a deep breath as she opened the door.

It wasn't Neil.

A gray-haired gentleman stood there, peering at her through gold-rimmed glasses. Slight of build, his hair was thinning at the temples, and a summer jacket hung a little loose on his shoulders.

"I'm sorry to bother you," he apologized quickly. "I'm looking for an old friend of mine, Devanna Davenport."

"That's my aunt," Courtney assured him quickly.

His face brightened. "Oh, good. I was afraid I might have the wrong houseboat. I'm Harold Jensen."

"I'm sorry, she's not in right now, Mr. Jensen. But I'm expecting her back any time. Would you like to come in and wait for her?"

"Yes, thank you. I'm looking forward to seeing Devanna again. It's a pleasure to meet her niece."

The use of her aunt's first name and his warm tone suggested a personal acquaintance. Courtney was curious how "personal" it might have been. Her aunt had still been a young woman when her older husband died. Maybe there had been some men in her life during those years she chose to live away from the family.

"Please have a seat," Courtney offered, glad that she'd straightened up the room before she sat down with her book. Jamie was kicking happily on a baby blanket she'd spread out on the floor beside the couch.

Mr. Jensen smiled at the baby as he took a nearby chair. With old-fashioned politeness, he made all the proper inquiries about Jamie's name and how old he was. She was glad she'd dressed Jamie in a pretty blue romper suit with matching booties. She didn't have many chances to show him off.

"May I get you something to drink?" Courtney offered.

"No, thank you. I'm fine."

"I'm sure Aunt Devanna will be happy to see you," Courtney told him, even though she knew better than to try and predict Devanna's behavior. Her aunt might react to Mr. Jensen the way she had to Neil, all friendly and outgoing, or she might give him that cold, vacant stare that sent shivers rippling up Courtney's back.

Mr. Jensen sighed. "To tell the truth, I lost track of Devanna years ago. I worked for her late husband, and spent a lot of time in their California home. I was his personal accountant until he died," he said with a hint of pride. "I've always remembered how nice she was to me."

As Mr. Jensen shared his memories of Devanna, Courtney realized how much her aunt had changed from those happy days when her husband was alive.

"I was sorry when Devanna sold the California company after her husband's death, and moved to Seattle. I often wondered what happened to her." He pushed back his glasses. "I'm now an accountant for Ellsworth Real Estate and Investment."

"You are?" she asked in surprise. "I just met Neil Ellsworth a few days ago."

"A very nice young man. I worked for his father until he retired. Anyway, yesterday I was handling some papers on houseboat rentals. Imagine my surprise when I came across Devanna's name. I guess there's no question about it being the same Devanna Davenport?"

Courtney assured him that her aunt's personal history matched the one he'd described. Because the man seemed sincerely interested, Courtney shared a little bit about her aunt's withdrawal from family contact and her tendency to be a recluse. In a way, she wanted to prepare him for meeting the withdrawn, strange woman her aunt had become.

After waiting nearly an hour, Devanna still hadn't returned and Mr. Jensen decided not to wait any longer. Since Courtney had no idea where her aunt had gone, it was anybody's guess when she'd be back. Obviously disappointed, Mr. Jensen prepared to take his leave.

"Please tell her that I dropped by, and I'll be back to see her another time," he said. "It's been a pleasure chatting with you. Your aunt must be proud of you and the baby."

"Aunt Devanna loves Jamie," Courtney responded, wishing she could say the same affection extended to her. "I've enjoyed meeting you, Mr. Jensen. Please come again."

"Thank you. I certainly will."

She stood on the front deck as he crossed the narrow dock and climbed the steps. He drove away in a small white car. What a nice man. He'd helped her pass a lonely afternoon, and she looked forward to seeing him again.

When her aunt came back, nearly two hours later, Courtney eagerly told her about Mr. Jensen's visit.

Devanna just shrugged. "I don't even remember the man. And I doubt he remembers me that well, either."

Her aunt's crude dismissal startled Courtney. Several times her use of coarse expressions seemed incongruous with her aunt's background, and Courtney wondered where she'd picked up the roughness.

NEIL'S PRIDE CONTINUED to smart from Courtney's lackluster response about a second date. He concentrated on business and tried to shove her to the back of his mind. After all, there were plenty of numbers in his little black book if he got in the mood to date someone. Unfortunately, he had to pass by the houseboat on the lake road both coming and going to work, and he couldn't help thinking about her.

When his sister Maribeth provided the perfect excuse to see her again, he thought, why not. There was always the chance that if he saw her again, he'd get over the ridiculous attraction that kept her at the edge of his mind.

She was sitting alone on the front deck reading when he drove to the houseboat to see her. A sudden glow in her eyes when she saw him was encouraging. Maybe she regretted her cool reaction about a second date after all.

"How have you been?" he asked as he dropped into a chair beside her.

"Fine," she assured him after a slight hesitation.

"And Jamie? How is the baby?"

She brightened. "Great. I just put him down for his nap."

"And your aunt?"

Once again Courtney hesitated. "Devanna seems to keep busy. I'm not sure exactly what she finds to do, or where she goes."

"So you're here pretty much by yourself?"

She gave him a faint smile as if she knew exactly what he was leading up to. Maybe it was no surprise to her that he was back again. Was he as apparent as all that, Neil asked himself.

Aloud, he asked, "How would you like to make my sister, Maribeth, happy?"

She raised an eyebrow. "Your sister?"

"She's giving a birthday party for our twin brothers, Alex and Allen. They're both married with families, but Maribeth is the one who organizes all the parties. She asked me to bring someone, and I was hoping you and Jamie might be my date. It's the day after tomorrow."

"Oh, I don't know," Courtney responded quickly. A dozen reasons why she shouldn't go flooded her mind as quickly as her next breath.

"There'll be kids and babies all over the place. Utter confusion. Lots of food. Good humor and teasing. What do you say?"

For a minute, Courtney couldn't say anything. She was completely taken aback by the invitation. Family birthday parties were completely outside her sphere of experience. How would she fit in at such a gathering? The way Neil was smiling at her, she wanted to go more than anything. It wouldn't be a romantic date, she reassured herself, and she wouldn't have to leave Jamie.

"I…I think I would like to go."

"Great. It'll be a casual affair," he assured her. "Nothing fancy. Just a good time."

Courtney couldn't think of anything that sounded more wonderful. Every day she spent on the houseboat deepened her feelings of isolation and loneliness.

"Thanks for asking me…us," she laughingly corrected herself. "It will be Jamie's first venture out into Manitou society."

"Good, I'll pick you up about six o'clock."

When Courtney told her aunt about the birthday party and her invitation to go, Devanna seemed pleased. It was only when Courtney told her she'd be taking Jamie with her that her aunt objected furiously.

"No, that's a stupid idea! A baby doesn't have any business at some wild shindig where people are carousing around, acting like damn fools."

"It's not that kind of party," Courtney protested. "It's a family get-together."

"You'll have a better time without him," Devanna said, trying a different tack. "No man wants to go out with a woman who's lugging around a baby."

"Neil specifically asked me to bring Jamie," Courtney countered. "There'll be other mothers and babies there."

Courtney had never seen her aunt angry before. Devanna said something under her breath. Her face was flushed. Her eyes had narrowed to almost slits.

She looked as if she were about to tell Courtney that she couldn't take Jamie.

Courtney just faced her with steady eyes and a firm chin. When it came to Jamie, nobody was going to tell her what she could and couldn't do.

With apparent effort, her aunt seemed to restrain herself, and said with a tight mouth, "I just want what's best for him."

"So do I," Courtney replied shortly, but the anguish in her aunt's face made her add gently, "Jamie is blessed to have an aunt who loves him so much. But he's *my* child."

Devanna turned away, went into her room and slammed the door.

THE NIGHT OF THE PARTY, Devanna didn't come out to speak to Neil when he came to pick up Courtney and the baby.

"Here we go, fellow," he said as he deftly fastened the belts across Jamie's carrier. Courtney could tell he hadn't exaggerated his uncle Neil role. He handled the baby like a pro. Neil glanced at Courtney as they drove through Manitou to his sister's home in a lovely residential area on the west end of the lake. She looked lovely in a simple, pale pink summer dress, tiny pearl earrings her only jewelry, and her hair pulled up on top of her head, with wisps of fair hair curling around her tanned cheeks. He felt a tightness in his chest just looking at her.

He couldn't tell from her tense expression if she was nervous about the evening, or unhappy about something. He wondered if she'd changed her mind about going out with him again. He'd never felt as unsure of himself with any woman as he did with her.

"Are you worried about something?" he finally asked, when every attempt he made at light conversation fell flat. Was she bored with his company already?

"It's my aunt," she sighed. "She threw a fit about me bringing Jamie. I can't help wondering if maybe she was right."

"Oh, so that's it." He smiled in relief. "A nervous mother. Believe me, you don't have a thing to worry about. Maribeth will love you both on sight—and so will everybody else."

"Tell me about your brothers. Are they identical twins?" she asked, wanting to keep the attention off herself. She wasn't at all sure that Neil's optimistic assurances weren't more hopeful thinking than anything.

"Yes, but they're different personalities and work together very well. They're partners in a successful car dealership." He chuckled. "Alex is the more aggressive. He'll probably try to sell you his latest model if you give him an opening."

When they arrived at a well-lit, two-storied home on the lake frontage, Neil held the baby's carrier in one hand and guided Courtney into the house with the other.

"We're here!"

Courtney scarcely had time to take a deep breath before she was enveloped in a sea of introductions to Neil's family and friends. She got the impression that they were totally surprised that he was arriving with a woman and a baby, and she was sure the absence of a wedding ring on her finger didn't go unnoticed.

"How nice to meet you, Courtney," Maribeth said, squeezing her hand. Short, dark, curly hair framed her face and accented the same shade of brown eyes as Neil's. She was rather plump, vivacious, and bubbled with friendliness. "And what a beautiful baby." She nodded at Neil and winked. "Nice going, brother!"

"I thought you'd approve," Neil answered, giving her an affectionate hug.

"Come on, Courtney, I'll show you the nursery." Maribeth took the carrier, then told her brother, "There's food and drink on the terrace, and some of the fellows are watching a football game. We'll make sure this little fellow is settled in, and then we'll be down."

"Sounds good." He winked at Courtney. "Don't get lost. My sister has a habit of monopolizing people she likes."

"It's true," Maribeth laughingly admitted as she and Courtney went upstairs. "Neil never said boo about who he was bringing. What a lovely surprise. I didn't know he was even seeing someone with a baby."

Courtney wanted to correct the "seeing" part, but Maribeth didn't give her a chance. A proud mother of a two-month-old little girl and a five-year-old boy, Maribeth centered the conversation on the demands and marvels of motherhood as she led the way down the upper hall.

"My son is playing with some of his cousins in the backyard. He thinks he's much too big to stay in the nursery," she said, laughing proudly.

Courtney tried to hide her shock when she saw the nursery. She couldn't believe the spacious, beautifully decorated room was the domain of one little baby girl in a ruffled pink bassinet. White furniture and carpet blended with lovely swags of lace curtains at the windows, and harmonized with a pastel floral wallpaper. The wonderful, clean smell was a sharp contrast to the stale odors in the houseboat's tiny quarters.

A large middle-aged woman in a nursemaid's uniform stood at a small kitchenette in the far corner of the room. As they entered, she turned around and asked, smiling, "Another little one for the party?"

"Yes, Hazel," Maribeth answered. "This cute fellow is going to keep Annette company."

The nursemaid tickled Jamie under the chin as she took him out of the carrier. He rewarded her attention with one of his toothless smiles.

"What a darling," she cooed. Nodding toward the diaper bag Courtney was carrying, she said, "I suspect there's everything I need in there to keep him happy while you enjoy yourself."

"He's been fed, and if you give him his pacifier, he'll probably drop off to sleep."

As Hazel settled Jamie in a crib, Maribeth drew Courtney over to the pink bassinet. "This is Annette."

Courtney gazed down at the sleeping baby girl dressed in a soft pink dress. "She's beautiful. And look at all that lovely dark hair. I keep waiting for Jamie's blond fuzz to thicken up."

They began sharing some of the trials and joys of being mothers, and a half an hour sped by without either of them realizing it.

"Oh, my goodness," Maribeth gasped when she heard the faint ring of a doorbell. "I'd better get back downstairs to my guests."

Courtney was reluctant to leave the warm comfort of the nursery and the sleeping babies. Jamie had contentedly let the pacifier drop from his mouth, closed his eyes and fallen asleep. She knew he was in good hands, but lately, she'd felt a growing undefined anxiety about him. She'd gotten in the habit of checking him several times at night and nap time to reassure herself that he wasn't getting sick. Her aunt had accused her of trying to smother Jamie with so much attention and seemed resentful that Courtney kept such a close watch on him.

Courtney's hesitation to leave the nursery must have been evident because Hazel assured her, "I'll call you if he isn't happy without his mommy."

"Neil's going to chew me out for keeping you upstairs so long," Maribeth said as they hurried downstairs.

The family party was in full swing inside the house and outside on the terrace. Guests flowed around a loaded buffet table or sat at scattered tables overlooking the lake. Courtney didn't see Neil anywhere and felt self-conscious mingling with a crowd of strangers.

Maribeth introduced Courtney to her husband, Richard. He was a tall, rather serious-looking man who seemed to enjoy his wife's bubbling personality. Courtney learned that he was an attorney. Obviously a successful one, Courtney decided, if he was able to afford the lovely home and paid help Maribeth seemed to take for granted.

"I'd better check on the food, and make sure we have enough of everything," Maribeth said.

"May I help with something?" Courtney asked as she followed her into a beautiful, spacious kitchen.

Maribeth quickly looked over counters loaded with trays of food and nodded in satisfaction. "I wonder if we ordered enough beer and wine. I'd better check."

As she disappeared into a butler's pantry, Courtney became aware of two young women sitting at a round table in a kitchen alcove. She was surprised when one of them waved at her.

"Come join us," a pretty plump blonde called out. "We're the wives of the birthday boys, and enjoying our own private celebration. Would you like some wine? I'm Peggy, and this is Hollie."

"Nice to meet you both. I'm Courtney. I came with Neil."

"We know." Peggy's eyes sparkled over the rim of her wine goblet. "Our brother-in-law is full of surprises."

"Why do you say that?" Courtney asked as she sat down and took the glass of wine that Hollie had poured for her. "Doesn't Neil usually bring someone to these family affairs?"

"Oh, indeed," Peggy answered. "Our brother-in-law is quite the swinging bachelor. Always got some good-looking gal in tow."

"But he never shows up with the same gal twice," Hollie volunteered. "I've never seen a man so afraid of getting seriously involved."

"We all thought Neil would be the first one married. He's two years older than our husbands, the twins." Peggy lowered her voice. "He got engaged when he was eighteen."

Hollie sent Peggy a warning glance. "I don't think we should go into all that."

"Why not?" She shrugged. "It's no secret. He put a ring on her finger when they were high-school seniors."

"That's too young to get engaged," Courtney said evenly, hoping to learn as much about Neil's romantic background as she could.

"It is," Hollie agreed.

"But Neil had been in love with Wendy all through high school," Peggy argued. "They made plans to go to the same college, and be married as soon as they could swing the finances. They even had their kids' names picked out. It was a damn dirty shame the way things turned out."

"What happened?" Courtney asked as casually as she could. She couldn't help but encourage any sharing that would give her insight into Neil's past.

"So sad," Peggy answered, draining the last sip of her wine. "Wendy died of leukemia before she was twenty-one."

"Neil's heart was broken—"

"And he's never found someone to mend it," Peggy said, finishing Hollie's sentence. "It's been ten years and he's still playing the field." She eyed

Courtney with open speculation. "He's never been able to put the past to rest. Neil has a reputation of love 'em and leave 'em."

Very politely, but doggedly, Peggy and Hollie asked Courtney some questions about herself and how she met Neil.

"I'm spending the summer with my aunt. She's rented a houseboat from Neil's company," Courtney said briefly. She wasn't about to fuel the gossip line.

"Speak of the devil," Peggy said affectionately as Neil came into the kitchen and spied the three women at the table.

"So this is where you're hiding out?" he chided. "I've been all over this house looking for you."

"Down, boy," Peggy teased. "I bet you've been drinking beer with the guys, and gawking at the football game."

Neil made a playful swipe at her. "That's what I love about you, Peggy. You always think the worst of me."

"No, I just know what a handsome rogue you are."

Neil held out his hand to Courtney. "Come on, let's hit the buffet and I'll tell you some good stories about these two gals."

As they left the kitchen, Courtney said, "I like them."

"They're both great gals. I'm glad you had a chance to meet them, but I'm claiming you for the rest of the evening."

Neil was attentive as they enjoyed a lavish buffet dinner on the terrace. They sat on a garden step instead of at one of the crowed tables.

"This is nice," she said, leaning back on her arms and looking at the lovely garden and deep green lawn. She took in deep breaths of the fresh evening air.

"What are you smiling about? Your eyes give you away, you know," Neal said as he studied them. "Sometimes they're guarded and hard. Right now, they're soft and misty like a spring sky."

As his tender gaze settled on her, she was thankful that she'd been warned not to be drawn into any fantasies about him. What kind of signals had she been giving out? She wasn't about to sign up as one of his conquests.

Someone brought a boom box out on the terrace, and immediately several couples started dancing, cheered on by enthusiastic spectators.

"How about it?" Neil asked, a glint of a challenge in his smile.

"What?"

"Do you like to dance?"

"No…yes," she contradicted herself. "But I'm not very good."

"I bet you're much too modest. Come on. Let's find out. I'll be an impartial judge."

"Proceed at your own risk," she said recklessly, ignoring that curious eyes centered on them.

As Neil pulled her to him, Courtney cradled into the graceful length of his body with perfect ease. She was glad the music was one of those slow "My baby done me wrong" ballads.

He held her so close that laying her cheek against his was a given. She lost herself in the hypnotic movement as he deftly guided her steps, and when the music stopped she felt a sense of loss.

As they pulled away from each other, he said solemnly, "Just as I thought. You lied."

The next song had just started when Neil was summoned to the telephone.

"Sorry," he apologized to Courtney.

"It's okay. I'll slip up and check on Jamie."

They went inside the house together. He stopped at the den and she went on upstairs. Both babies were sound asleep, and Hazel assured her that all was well.

When Courtney came back downstairs, the door to the den was slightly ajar and she could hear Neil shouting in a rage.

"Don't you threaten me! You made your bed, lie in it! You try anything, and I'll have your ass in a sling." He swore as he slammed down the receiver. The fury in his voice dismayed her. He'd always seemed so even tempered, and it frightened her to realize how little she really knew him.

When he came out of the den, she pretended to be just coming down the stairs.

"Jamie's fussy," she lied. "I think we'd better call it an evening."

He didn't argue.

Conversation was sparse between them on the way back to the houseboat, and it was apparent to Courtney that Neil was still upset over the telephone call. When she boldly asked him what was the matter, he responded flatly. "Bad business."

His tone didn't invite any more questions.

At the door of the houseboat, she thanked him politely for the evening and said, "I enjoyed meeting your family."

"Thanks for coming." He lightly kissed her cheek. "I'm sorry about the bad mood. Forgive me?"

"Sure. I've had a few of those myself."

As his steps faded away, Courtney locked the door and quickly made her way through the darkened houseboat. Her aunt's door was closed and there were no audible sounds. As quickly as she could, Courtney settled Jamie for the night and got ready for bed.

As she lay there going over the evening's events, she could hear the wind rising, and the rocking motion of the waves increase. The moon was shrouded in dark clouds and a rumbling warned of an approaching storm. Oh, no, she thought. I'm going to be trapped inside for another endless day.

She was still wide-awake when she had a sense of another presence. At first she thought it was her imagination. Then a movement of air hit her face. She sat up with a jerk.

Devanna was bending over the baby.

"What are you doing?"

"He's crying. I'm going to take him to bed with me. He's cold."

"He's not crying, and he's not cold." Courtney swung down from the bed. "You leave him where he is."

"No, he wants me! Can't you tell?"

Courtney pushed herself between her aunt and the bassinet. "The baby is fine. Don't bother him."

A flash of lightning lit up her aunt's face, and Courtney was stunned. Her aunt looked angry enough to attack her.

"You must have had a bad dream," Courtney said quickly and as soothingly as her tense voice would allow. "Everything's all right. Go back to bed."

Devanna didn't move. Courtney heard her say something under her breath, but couldn't make it out. Suddenly a clap of deafening thunder shook the walls of the houseboat. The whole floor seemed to drop away from under their feet.

Slowly Devanna backed out of the room. She disappeared in the darkness, and a moment later, her compartment door shut with an angry bang.

"Thank God." *What if I'd been asleep?*

Courtney hugged herself to stop the shivers. From now on, she'd keep her door locked at night.

If she hadn't heard Devanna, the older woman might have stealthily slipped Jamie out of his bassinet without her knowing it. And in her confused state, no telling what she would have done with or to the baby.

Chapter Four

All night the houseboat rocked in the undulating surf, pulling at its creaking mooring chains as a storm system slipped down from Canada and into the northern Idaho mountains. The very walls of the floating house seemed ready to give way at any moment against the onslaught.

The next morning the outside decks were soaked, and sprays of water whipped against the windows, shutting out the cloud-shrouded sunlight. Courtney's escape from the confining inside quarters of the houseboat was completely shut off. The day was long and tedious.

Jamie picked up on Courtney's nervous energy, and tried her patience with short naps and constant fussing.

"I told you that you shouldn't have taken him out last evening," Devanna declared. "He probably picked up something. It'll be your fault if he comes down sick."

Courtney held her temper. What good would it do to argue? All her efforts to create a harmonious relationship between them seemed doomed to failure. The only bonding between them was the baby, and now that was unraveling. Nothing was said about last night's confrontation and Courtney wondered if her aunt had been walking in her sleep.

"I guess this would be a good day to read," Courtney said. "Is there a book you'd recommend?"

"I haven't read any of them."

"What about your embroidery? You could work on that."

"And put my eyes out?" she scoffed.

Courtney gave up. "What does the radio say about the storm ending?"

"Radio? I don't have a radio. Where'd you get an idea like that?"

Courtney started to challenge her, but decided against saying anything. Lying about the radio was another of Devanna's little quirks. It was obvious that she hated sharing, and it was a mystery to Courtney why her aunt had invited her to come stay in the first place.

The long day dragged on. The wind created a keening sound as it whipped high waves against the sides of the houseboat. It sounded as if a hundred wailing creatures were beating to get inside. Wavering gray sunlight gave way to deepening twilight and night shadows.

Sharing the care of Jamie had been the only salvation of a long, nerve-racking day, and Courtney didn't know how she could take another day being cooped up with Devanna. She was wide-awake at midnight when the storm began to slacken, and by three o'clock she was finally able to fall asleep.

Jamie woke her up at five o'clock for an early bottle. Wearily, Courtney put on jeans and a warm sweater to hold off a chill that the storm had brought, and kept a blanket around the baby as she fed him

For some reason, Devanna stayed in her room until nearly ten o'clock.

"How'd our baby sleep?" she asked when she got up.

"He woke up early, and went back to sleep after his bottle."

"I thought I heard him crying. I was going to get up and tend to him if he kept it up," she warned, as if she wasn't going to let Courtney interfere the way she had the last time.

"That's sweet of you, Aunt Devanna, but you don't need to be so concerned about him. You need your sleep." There was an edge to her tone, but her aunt didn't seem to notice.

Devanna seemed preoccupied as she poured a cup of coffee. She was dressed in the plain brown slacks and pullover she usually wore when she went out.

Courtney was busy getting Jamie's laundry ready for the washer when there was a knock at the door.

"You didn't order any groceries for today, did you?" Devanna demanded as she went to answer it. "I'm not paying for all the extra stuff you're buying."

Courtney bit back a tart reply as her aunt opened the door, and froze with a baby blanket in her hand when she heard Neil's cheery voice.

"Just thought I'd check on you ladies, and see how you weathered the storm."

"My goodness, you didn't need to put yourself out

like that," Devanna said quickly. "We'd stayed nice and dry. No damage to the houseboat at all."

"That's good news."

"I guess you're busy checking on all your renters." Devanna made no move to invite him in.

"Only the special ones."

Courtney came over to the door. "Won't you come in, Neil?"

"Oh, yes, please do," Devanna said quickly, stepping back. "We don't have handsome gentlemen calling on us very often. I forgot my manners."

Courtney ignored her aunt's chatter as her eyes settled on Neil. He wore a tan raincoat, and his wavy, dark hair glistened with moisture. She felt a surging warmth just looking at him.

"What a nice surprise," Courtney said.

"I'm not interrupting anything?"

"Not at all."

She had played the birthday party over and over again in her mind, and even toyed with the idea of dropping by his office. She wasn't sure he was interested in pursuing any relationship, but here he was, using the storm as an excuse to come by.

"I was just starting the baby's washing."

"She's such a good little mother," Devanna said unexpectedly with a notable lack of warmth in the compliment.

"Yes, I know." He smiled at Courtney. "My sister was very impressed with her and the baby. And so was I."

Courtney felt her cheeks grow warm as he centered arresting brown eyes on her.

"Would you like some coffee?" Devanna asked rather abruptly, as if she didn't like the way the conversation was going.

"Thanks. It's supposed to warm up, but there's a chill in the air this morning."

He sat down on the couch and Courtney took a place beside him, letting her aunt do the honors of getting the coffee.

"There's been a lot of damage from the high waters. The morning paper is full of unfortunate damage. And deaths." A shadow crossed his face. "Some of them quite close to home."

"Not anyone in your family?" Courtney asked quickly, her chest tightening.

"Not immediate family," he assured her. "One of my employees, Harold Jensen."

Courtney put a hand up to her throat. "Oh, no."

"You knew him?" Neil gave her a look of total surprise.

"I…I didn't really know him, but Aunt Devanna did. He came by to see her just the other day." Courtney shot a look at her aunt. "Mr. Jensen worked for your late husband, didn't he, Devanna?"

"Not that I remember," she answered flatly.

Neil looked puzzled. "Jensen must have remembered you, Devanna. Why would he take the time to look you up? How did he know you were here?"

Devanna shrugged and continued to look disinterested in the conversation.

"He said he was working for your company." Courtney repeated what Jensen had told her. "He saw the rental records on the houseboats, and recog-

nized the name. He wasn't sure he had the right Devanna Davenport, but what he told me matched my
aunt's background."

"And you had a good visit with him?" Neil asked
Devanna.

"I wasn't here when he came by," she answered
with a disinterested shrug. "Courtney told me about
him, but he never came back."

"He was very friendly," Courtney said, remembering the man's gentle caring way. "How did he die?"

"His body washed up on the far end of the lake
during last night's storm."

"He drowned?" Courtney gasped.

"No, he didn't die from drowning." Neil's jaw
tightened and his eyes darkened. "Jensen was shot."

"Shot?" Courtney echoed as if she wasn't sure
she'd heard correctly.

"How could such a thing happen?" Devanna
asked, watching Neil's face carefully.

"The police aren't sure. They don't know how
long his body has been in the water—but not long.
Jensen didn't have any next of kin, so they called me
to identify the body." Neil's voice thickened with
emotion. "He was the nicest guy you'd ever want to
know."

"Did Jensen have money?" Devanna asked, her
eyes suddenly alive with interest. "Some people go
around without a dime in their pockets, but have a
bank account that would choke a horse."

"No." Neil shook his head. "Jensen lived mod-
estly. The police are baffled about a motive."

"He might have been in the wrong place at the

wrong time," Devanna offered. "It happens that way sometimes."

"I'm really sorry, Neil," Courtney said gently, and impulsively took his hand. It was obvious Neil had a deep affection for the deceased man. "Is there anything we can do?"

"I'm not sure. He doesn't have a close family. I'm the one who will have to make arrangements as soon as the police release the body."

"How soon will that be?"

"There'll be a complete investigation. Unless he committed suicide, someone killed him and dumped his body in the lake."

Courtney frowned. "He didn't seem the least bit despondent to me. He gave the impression he was enjoying life."

"I don't believe for a minute that he killed himself." Neil straightened his shoulders as if fighting back a surge of anger. "Well, I guess I'd better get back to the office. If you two are all right—"

"We're fine," Courtney assured him. "I'm very sorry about Mr. Jensen's tragic end."

"It's a mystery, isn't it?" Devanna commented with a knowing nod.

"I'll tell Detective McGrady that you visited with Jensen recently, Courtney. He may want to talk with you. Something that Jensen said might be of help."

"I can't think of anything, but I'd be glad to answer his questions."

"Good," he said and turned to leave.

"Come again," Devanna invited in one of her rare efforts at hospitality.

Something in her eyes didn't echo the invitation, and Courtney knew with certainty that for some reason her aunt did not like Neil.

"I'll walk out to the steps with you," Courtney offered. She didn't want him going away without some personal exchange between them. Just seeing him again had ignited feelings she'd been trying to dismiss in her daydreams about him. Common sense told her she'd been warned not to get involved, but when he gave her that engaging smile, she forgot to be sensible.

Once out of her aunt's hearing, Neil ordered, "Tell me the truth now. What's going on with you? You look beat down to a stub."

"I didn't do well handling the storm. I hated being shut in close quarters. The heavy downpour and constant motion got on my nerves."

As she looked around, she couldn't believe how high the houseboat was floating on the water. She shivered. What if the mooring chain had given way and the houseboat had been sent crashing against the shoreline?

"There's no need to be scared," he quickly reassured her, seeing a flicker of fright in her eyes. "You're safe enough inside the houseboat."

"I've never been around water very much. A city swimming pool is challenge enough for me, and I only tried it a couple of times." She felt a little foolish that she'd expressed her fears.

"You seemed to enjoy taking a spin in my boat," he reminded gently, trying to lighten her mood. Growing up in Manitou, water was such a part of his life, he couldn't imagine someone being terrified of it.

"Oh, I did enjoy myself," she assured him. "I think the constant floating sensation beneath my feet wears me down." She paused. "And there's just something about the houseboat that I can't quite define. I think it's well named, *Nevermore*. That's the way I feel about it."

"Living on the water is a different experience," he agreed. "But nothing to be afraid of."

She visibly straightened her shoulders. "My imagination runs away from me sometimes. My mother used to say that I had a sixth sense about things when I was a little girl, and ever since I got here, I've been fighting some inner apprehension that I can't quite define." She gave a deprecating laugh. "I suppose it has something to do with my being a new mother. It's natural, I guess, to worry whether you're doing the right thing or not."

"It can't be easy raising a child on your own," he observed. "But from what I see of Jamie, he seems to be thriving. And it's obvious your aunt is willing to help with the baby. Why don't you relax, and let her take over more?"

"I guess I should," Courtney admitted. "She's ready and willing any time I ask her." *Even when I don't ask her.*

"What is it?" he asked, seeing her frown.

"I think my aunt's deep attachment to Jamie is interfering with her sleep. The other night she imagined that she heard him crying, and she got up in the middle of the night to get him. Either that, or she's sleepwalking. I've decided to keep my door locked."

"Probably a good idea," he agreed. "I have to agree that your aunt's a bit of a puzzle."

"Thanks for coming. I...I really appreciate it."

"Maribeth would like to see you again—and so would I."

A pleased smile hovered on her lips, and he was tempted to pull her close, but before he could give in to the temptation, she stepped back.

She didn't say anything, but he got the message. Her pleasure in seeing him wasn't going to be a green light for any romantic advances. Normally, he would have shrugged it off. He'd enjoyed the friendship of many women he'd never dated romantically, and it certainly made sense to include Courtney in that category. The problem was, he didn't feel very sensible. Just being with her stirred desires that went beyond platonic.

He cleared his throat and said as casually as he could, "Goodbye then. And anytime you need anything, let me know. That's what friends are for. Agreed?"

"I could use a friend." Courtney wondered if it would be possible to enjoy a friendly relationship with Neil and still remain free of a tangled romantic situation that could break her heart. Falling for Neil Ellsworth had all kinds of Danger signs posted around it.

"Good. It's settled then. I'll be in touch. Once I've finalized arrangements for Jensen, I'll let you know, in case you'd like to go."

"Yes, I would very much like to pay my respects."

A funeral wasn't exactly Neil's idea of the perfect

date, but he was glad there would be an occasion to see Courtney again.

As he drove back to the office, he couldn't help but wonder why Jensen made an effort to see Devanna when she denied remembering him. He had been a quiet man who lived simply and privately. The thought that someone would shoot him and dump his body in the lake was unbelievable, and Neil's hands tightened on the steering wheel just thinking about it.

When Courtney went back in the houseboat, Devanna was getting ready to take off in her van again.

"Going shopping?"

"Don't need anything," the older woman answered flatly.

She never brought back any packages, or asked Courtney if she needed anything picked up from the stores. What she did with her time away from the houseboat was a mystery.

Even though Courtney could have taken drives in her own car, the long trip to Manitou had blunted her pleasure in being behind the wheel. Also, there was the matter of spending money unnecessarily on gas. The drain on her finances was already more than she had expected. Devanna never seemed to be around when the groceries were delivered.

NEIL WAS IN HIS OFFICE, a few days later, when Detective McGrady came in to see him. He was a ruddy-faced, middle-aged man who was tall and loose-jointed. He looked as if he might have his horse tethered around the corner of the building. His relaxed manner gave the impression he had all the time in the world to listen to anything anyone had to say. A family man with six children of his own, McGrady had the trust of the community when it came to handling out-of-control youths, or getting to the bottom of more serious crimes.

"Hope I'm not interrupting anything."

"Not at all. Have a seat," Neil offered, anxious to find out what, if anything, the detective had learned about Jensen's death.

As McGrady sat down in a chair, he spread his long legs out in front of him and gazed around the office. "You've fixed it up since your dad had it. I remember coming in here when our first kid was born."

Neil wasn't fooled. All the homey chat was just a warm-up. He smiled and waited.

"Well, now, this whole thing about Jensen is a shocker, isn't it? Everybody says he was a real nice guy."

"He was," Neil said firmly.

"Not an enemy in the world? Is that what you're saying? Interesting?" He rubbed his chin. "Well, then he must have shot himself somehow, and the storm pulled his body out into the lake."

"I don't believe it. No, he didn't commit suicide. Jensen was more well-adjusted and satisfied with life than anyone else in the office. He was always calming the rest of us when we got in a rage."

"Well, now that leaves us with a bit of a puzzle, doesn't it?"

"Who in the world would want to shoot a nice guy like Harold?" Neil shook his head. "None of it makes sense. He didn't have any enemies. It must have been an accidental shooting."

"An accident, eh? I guess we'll know when the coroner's report comes in." McGrady seemed to ponder the idea. "How do you think a thing like that could happen?"

"Perhaps he was with someone, maybe they were cleaning guns, and one went off."

"And then what?" McGrady gently prodded.

Neil knew he was grasping at straws, but he couldn't bring himself to believe that someone would deliberately point a gun at Jensen and shoot the man to death.

"Whoever was with him got scared," Neil speculated. "Thought he might be accused, and decided to dump the body in the lake, and remain quiet."

"Mmm, know anybody who was a hunting buddy of Jensen's?"

"That's what's puzzling. Harold talked a lot about going fishing, but I can't remember him mentioning hunting. Other people in the office might. He was friendly with everyone. Went out of his way to be nice to people." Neil thought about Jensen's visit to see Devanna—who didn't even remember him. He started to mention it to McGrady, but the detective's pager went off before he could.

McGrady listened, and his relaxed, easygoing manner disappeared. He was instantly on his feet, and headed out of the office. "Robbery. Capital Bank around the corner."

As the detective bolted out of the building, Neil tried to keep up with his long stride. A small branch bank stood on the corner of a busy intersection a block away.

When they reached the scene, McGrady darted inside the bank while Neil remained outside. The parking lot was full of cars, and policemen on foot were canvassing all the vehicles. Almost immediately, there was a traffic jam as the word spread that the police were checking every car and pedestrian in the area.

No suspects were picked up. Neil returned to the office without seeing McGrady again.

The evening news broadcast gave a detailed account of the robbery. A videotape showed a man with gray hair and full mustache, wearing a cowboy hat, entering the bank almost as soon as it opened.

The newscaster reported that the police believed the robber was familiar with the routine because he waited until the security guard was getting his usual cup of coffee before he came up behind him and silently dropped the guard with a gun butt to the head.

Two cashiers and one customer weren't even aware of the unfolding drama until the robber flashed his gun, and successfully made his escape with a shopping bag filled with money.

Watching a clip of the video on television, Neil had a strange feeling there was something familiar about the man's figure, but he couldn't recall having seen him before.

HUMMING THE SONG *"Happy Days Are Here Again,"* *she sat in front of the small locker, and returned a gray wig, mustache and Buzz's cowboy hat. After emptying out the shopping bag, she began counting bundles of money. The haul was more than she'd hoped for.*

She laughed excitedly. "Now I can get on the move again. It's time."

Buzz agreed with her. He reminded her that the unexpected discovery of Jensen's body could be a problem if the police discovered he'd made a second visit to see Devanna.

Smiling, she hugged herself. As soon as she could arrange things, she'd disappear again, and this time she'd have their baby boy with her.

Chapter Five

After Neil made arrangements for Harold Jensen's burial at the Chapel on the Hill mortuary and cemetery, he advised Courtney that he'd be happy to drive her and Devanna to the services.

"You go," Devanna told Courtney when they discussed the matter. "I'll babysit."

"Are you sure?" Courtney couldn't understand her aunt's complete indifference to a man who'd taken the trouble to come and see her. She had showed no interest at all in his tragic death and waved aside any discussion of it.

"Of course, I'm sure." She bent over the baby, cooing, "You want to stay here with me, don't you, cutie-pie?"

Courtney hesitated. She'd never been comfortable going off and leaving Jamie with just anybody. But, of course, Devanna was family, Courtney reminded herself, and clearly devoted to the baby.

Obviously, Jamie would be better off staying at the houseboat with Devanna if she really didn't want to go. Courtney had been a little worried about managing him at the funeral anyway.

Services were scheduled for ten o'clock in the morning, and Neil came by at nine o'clock to pick her up. She'd been wavering about what she should wear, and finally settled on dark blue slacks and a matching fitted tunic. She wore a simple gold necklace and tiny earrings, and her fair hair pulled back into a smooth twist.

"Are you two and the baby ready?" Neil asked, as his warm glance of approval traveled over her.

She was startled at how handsome he looked in a tailored dark suit, white shirt with gold cuff links and maroon tie. His dark hair had been styled in a shorter, layered cut that emphasized his brown eyes.

"Oh, my aunt's not going," Courtney replied quickly. "She's going to babysit Jamie."

"That's right." Devanna nodded.

Neil slapped his forehead in an exasperated gesture. "Didn't I tell you that Maribeth was planning on keeping Jamie? I bet I didn't." He groaned. "Maribeth's going to blow a fuse. She wanted to help out. Everything's been arranged to drop Jamie off there while we attend services."

"Well, then, I guess we'd better pretend you told me," Courtney said, smiling. "Just give me a couple of minutes and I'll get his things together."

Devanna's face turned an ugly red. "Why haul Jamie around to some strange place when he's fine here?" she lashed out. "There's absolutely no need to take him anywhere. He's better off staying with me."

Courtney stiffened at her aunt's aggressive behavior. This wasn't the first time they'd clashed over her display of possessiveness. More and more Devanna had begun to ignore Courtney when it came to making decisions about handling the baby.

"Since Maribeth has made arrangements to keep him, we'll leave him there," Courtney said firmly and ignored her aunt's seething displeasure.

"I'm sorry about that," Neil apologized as they drove away from the houseboat with Jamie in his carrier in the back seat. "I didn't mean to get you at odds with your aunt."

"It's not your fault," Courtney sighed. "I guess I'm just not used to handling family relationships. Sometimes my aunt's devotion to Jamie is too much of a good thing. I'm glad she loves him, and wants to take care of him, but I'm completely baffled why I can't seem to establish any kind of a relationship with her. The few letters I got from her were so different. I can't figure out from her distant behavior why she wanted me to come here in the first place."

"I don't know, but I'm glad she did," Neil answered readily, smiling at her as he reached over and touched her hand. "This is where you say, 'Me too.'"

The softness in his eyes sent her emotions on a roller coaster. His touch instantly wiped out all the lectures she'd been giving herself about keeping her distance during the outing. How could she resist his charm? He had a way of making her feel special. She smiled back and readily echoed, "Me, too."

When they stopped at his sister's house to leave

the baby, Maribeth seemed sincerely delighted to see Courtney again.

"Now don't you give Jamie a second thought. Hazel and I will treat him like His Royal Highness," she promised.

Neil glanced at his watch. "We'd better get going. The steep road up to the Chapel on the Hill is a slow one."

"But it's a beautiful drive," Maribeth assured her. "The view is spectacular. You can see clear across the lake to the far ridge of mountains. Takes your breath away."

Courtney had to agree. As the winding road climbed the side of the mountain, every view out the window was awesome. When they reached a beautiful mountain meadow on a high bluff, she could see why Neil had chosen this place for Jensen's remains. Quiet, serene, the setting was perfect.

Services were held in the white picturesque chapel, bordered by a cemetery landscaped by natural mountain beauty. Only a handful of people attended, most of them from Neil's office, but there was a genuine expression of affection for the man who had met death by an unseen hand.

Neil remained for a few minutes after the service to speak to the funeral director, and they were one of the last to leave. Courtney could tell Neil was deeply affected by Harold's death.

"Thanks for coming," he told her in a strained voice. "I know Harold would have appreciated it."

She slipped her hand into his, holding it tightly as they made their way back to the car. She blinked back a sudden fullness in her eyes. "I'm glad you asked me."

"We could stop somewhere and have lunch before we pick up the baby." The funeral had left him with a mixture of grief and anger, and he didn't want to be alone. He knew he wouldn't have to pretend, or entertain Courtney. He'd felt her sincere empathy during the services.

As they made their way down the winding mountain road, Courtney gazed out the window, drawing in the beauty of the dark green mountain etched against a cloudless blue sky. For the first time since arriving in Manitou, she was able to center in the peace of the moment, and—

There was no warning. Gunfire shattered the air as they came around a sharp curve. Tires on the car exploded.

"What the hell?" Neil cried as he lost control.

Courtney screamed as the car plunged off the side of the road, crashing down a steep rocky incline, bucking and groaning, and heading for a steep drop-off that fell hundreds of feet below. The car plowed into a thick stand of ponderosa pines edging the deep chasm. By some miracle, several thick trunks withstood the force of the plunging car. They bent and splintered but kept the car from dropping off the cliff into the rocky ravine below as a roar of crumpled metal and shattered glass filled the air.

Courtney's breath was shoved back in her lungs as the force of the sudden stop ejected the air bags and pressed her and Neil back in their seats.

A weighted silence followed the ear-piercing crash. The only sound was the air bags deflating.

"Are you—are you—all right?" Neil finally stammered in a cracked voice.

After the horrendous scare, she wasn't sure about anything. "I…I think so."

Before Neil could straighten up and push the deflated air bag aside, a warning shiver of the car sent Neil's adrenaline racing.

Were the thick tree trunks giving way under pressure?

Courtney cried out as the car suddenly pitched slightly forward. Any second the trees could uproot and send the car sailing over the high cliff into midair.

"We've got to get out now." Neil struggled to open his door but it was wedged too close to one of the trees to budge. The side window was intact, but even if he could get it rolled down, he wouldn't be able to climb out because the tree trunk pinned him in.

"Can you open your door?"

She'd already tried. "Not very far. Some huge boulders are in the way."

Neil cursed his two-door car.

"Maybe I could squeeze out," Courtney said doubtfully, eyeing the opening of a few inches.

The car shifted again.

"Try! Now!" Neil's chest tightened. If even one tree trunk gave way, enough pressure could be put on the others to flatten them, and nothing else stood between the car and the edge of a thousand-foot drop to the rocky ravine below. Getting Courtney out was uppermost in his mind. As he looked at the narrow opening of her door, his heart sank. It didn't look wide enough for a small dog.

With prayerful breath, he watched her push and turn her slender body as she forced it through the narrow opening. When she was finally outside, he was weak with relief.

"Good girl!"

"Now it's your turn." As the words left her lips, she realized in horror that Neil would never be able to get his muscular frame through her door opening, and the window was partially blocked by a large boulder.

Even with Neil pushing on the door, and her pulling as hard as she could, they couldn't make the opening even an inch wider. She doubted that even a bulldozer would have an easy time of moving them.

"What'll we do?" she cried in panic. He had to get out!

"Get away from the car," he shouted back. If the car suddenly plunged forward, he didn't want her near it. With all the windows and the two doors blocked, there was only one possible exit open to him—the windshield.

Neil jerked opened the glove compartment and pulled out a flashlight. It was the only thing of any size he had to break glass. Covering his eyes with one hand, he swung at the windshield. The glass shattered from the blow, and some of it fell away, but he needed a bigger hole to crawl through.

At that instant, with a warning groan, one of the largest trees began to bend forward in slow motion.

"Get out! Get out!" Courtney cried.

Broken glass littered the dashboard and hood as Neil pounded at the edges of the hole then eased through the shattered opening. He slid off the car just as it began to move.

Neil grabbed Courtney as the car lurched forward. They frantically climbed up onto the pile of boulders, and clung together as the car dropped over the edge. They watched it tumble over and over, searing a path down the mountainside, and ending up as a mangled mass of metal far below.

Courtney buried her face against Neil's chest and he held her tightly. Her body shivered as if she had suddenly been dipped in ice. Her breath came in short gasps. Everything that had happened was like a runaway kaleidoscope in her mind. Shock coated the unreal, the unthinkable. It couldn't have happened. She could hear Neil murmuring reassurances but they seemed to come from far away.

"It's okay," he said easing her down off the pile of boulders.

"Why…why?" she sobbed.

He struggled to find an answer. Was the shooting the carelessness of a hunter or someone target practicing? He immediately rejected that explanation. The shots were not random. The shooter had been aiming at the car's tires. The target had been deliberate—and almost deadly.

"Some lunatic. It has to be," Neil answered shortly.

"Why would anyone do such a thing?"

"I don't know, but, by God, we'll find him."

"You've got a cut on your cheek. Your white shirt is bloody."

"Just scratches. How about you?"

Amazingly, they had only suffered a few cuts and bruises. Courtney's hair had fallen away from its pins, and her face was smudged with dirt. She had ripped her tunic when she squeezed through the door opening, but she was unhurt.

Neil's hands were nicked with bits of glass, and he had blood spots on his black trousers, and a sleeve on his jacket was torn.

All in all, they had escaped near-death almost unscathed.

"It could have been a lot worse," Courtney said, thankfully.

Neil refused to go there. What might have happened was a living nightmare that was going to be with them for a very long time. "Let's get out of here."

As he scanned the mountainside above them, he knew it wasn't going to be an easy climb. The slope was steep, and the rugged terrain was covered with patches of thorny shrubs and huge gray boulders that lined shelves of rough rocks. The car had flattened some of the smaller trees in its path and dislodged some of the rocks, but the distance up to the road was daunting.

Neil looked at Courtney's summer sandals, and silently groaned. Her feet would take a beating on the rough ground. His dress oxfords wouldn't be much better. This wasn't going to be a leisurely midday walk. They needed hiking boots to navigate the rough terrain.

"We'll go slowly, and stop to rest any time you want," he promised. "I'll lead, and try to find the easiest way. We won't be able to go up in a straight line," he warned.

"I'll keep up."

The defensive way she said it brought a smile to his face. "I never doubted it for a minute."

He wanted to thank her for not falling apart on him. He didn't know what he would have done if he'd had a hysterical woman with him in the car. Courtney had kept her head, and both of them were alive because of it.

They were forced to move horizontally to find a climbable passage upward, and the distance back to the road was tripled. Surging adrenaline from their narrow escape kept them climbing at a steady pace.

The sun, directly overhead, beat down on their heads and perspiring faces.

When they finally reached the road, Neil put up a warning hand to keep Courtney behind him. What assurance did they have that the gunman wasn't still concealed nearby?

"Do you think he's still here?" Courtney asked with a dry mouth.

Neil didn't answer. "There's a car coming. You stay here in the trees. I'll step out and stop it."

She grabbed his sleeve. "What if it's the shooter?"

"We'll have to chance it. If something goes wrong—you get the hell out of here. Understand?"

He stepped out of the trees and waited at the edge of the pavement for the car to come around the curve. His knees nearly buckled with relief when the vehicle came into view. It was the black hearse from the mortuary.

Stepping out into the road, Neil waved down the startled driver and called to Courtney that the coast was clear.

The startled young man gaped at their dirty, bloody appearance. "What happened?" His eyes widened with disbelief as they told him.

"You gotta be kidding. Some bozo shot up your car? Why'd he do a dumb thing like that?" He asked the question as if he expected Neil to give him rhyme and reason for the whole thing.

"I don't know, but we need a ride."

"Sure thing. We usually don't take live passengers in this buggy, but three people can squeeze in the front seat. Where do you want to go?"

Neil gave his address. On the drive back to town, he kept his arm around Courtney, thankful for the close quarters that kept her pressed close to him. He was feeling a little shaky himself.

"We'll call McGrady right away and tell him what happened. If the bastard is still roving around up there with a gun, the police might be able to catch him."

"Maybe I should go on to Maribeth's?"

"No," he said firmly. "We both need to get cleaned up first. If my sister sees us like this, she'd have a fit. I'm betting she'd call in the family doctor, and nothing we could say would stop her. You're okay, aren't you?" He searched Courtney's face. "I mean, we can go straight to the hospital—"

"No. I'm fine. You're right. No use getting her all

upset. I'll just call and warn her that I'll be a little late picking up Jamie."

Neil was glad he didn't have any close neighbors to see him emerge from a hearse with a woman on his arm. Luckily he still had his wallet, and gave the young man a big thank-you tip.

Courtney's heart sank when she realized her purse had gone over the cliff with the car. She'd just cashed a check a few days earlier, and the loss would throw her limited budget into a tailspin. Still, she was alive, and that put everything into a different perspective.

Once inside Neil's fashionable mountain home, he headed straight for the phone. "I'll call McGrady."

Courtney quickly decided that the modern house was designed for the independent lifestyle of a single man who valued his freedom. A high-ceilinged living room was furnished with ultra-modern furniture, soft beige carpets and large picture windows framed with leaf-green draperies. There was a casual, comfortable air that Courtney found inviting and appealing.

She followed Neil into a den complete with bar, leather lounge chairs and sofa, and an entertainment center that took up a whole wall. She suspected that the upstairs quarters were just as spacious. She listened as he reported to McGrady what had happened.

"Some idiot shot out our tires on that big curve just below the chapel... No, we didn't see anyone. Our car plunged off the road. Got caught by some huge trees or we'd be in the bottom of the ravine." He listened a minute. "Good. He may still be up there somewhere." He hung up and turned to Courtney. "He's sending some men up there, and he'll be right out to talk with us."

She nodded and stood there as if too dazed to say or do anything and he quickly put his arm around her. She looked like a refugee from a battle zone. Her arms were scratched and bruised. Thank God she hadn't been seriously hurt. Gently he brushed back the tangled strands of hair and smoothed the dirt smudges on her face.

"Come on, I'll show you the bathroom. You can freshen up a bit before McGrady gets here. I'll call Maribeth and explain why we'll be delayed in picking up Jamie."

He led her upstairs to a guest suite at the front of the house. "My rooms are down the hall," he said. "I think you'll find everything you need. Come on down when you're ready. I'll fix a couple of drinks for us. God knows we could use one."

The spacious sitting room, bedroom and adjoining bathroom were almost as big as the studio apartment she'd been renting in Cheyenne. Courtney took one look at herself in the fancy bathroom and groaned. Her face was scratched, her hair hanging in tangled strands around her face, and her best outfit dirty and torn. She cleaned up as best she could. She brushed her hair with a silver-plated brush and comb that had undoubtedly been used by more than one of Neil's female visitors.

When she heard the doorbell, she took a deep breath and went back downstairs. Neil was in the den with a lanky homespun-looking man.

"I'm sure sorry about all this," McGrady said as

Neil introduced her. "Why don't we sit down, and talk about what happened? Maybe we'll be lucky and this will all be behind us in short order."

"You hear about random shootings all the time," Neil said as he sat down close to Courtney on the leather sofa. "But I never thought I'd be one of the victims."

McGrady took a chair opposite them. He rested a notebook casually in his lap, as if he wasn't concerned about recording every word they said. He asked a few leading questions that encouraged them to talk freely.

"So you think the gunman was just doing a little target practice."

"It's the only thing that makes sense," Neil answered.

"There were quite a few cars on that road, weren't there? Because of the funeral, and all?"

Neil nodded. "We were the last ones to leave the chapel."

"He let all the other cars go by, and chose yours as his target," McGrady mused in his slow way. "I wonder why?"

Neil stiffened. "You don't think he was waiting especially to hit mine?"

McGrady frowned. "It's kind of a puzzle, isn't it? Do you know anyone who might want to take a pot-shot at you, Neil?"

Neil didn't answer right away. From the look on his face, he wasn't at all that sure what his answer should be. "Every businessman makes a few enemies now and then," he answered evasively.

"How about recently?" McGrady prodded in his quiet, dogged way.

Neil's expression darkened, and Courtney remembered the heated telephone call she'd overheard. The angry conversation he'd had with someone still rang in her ears.

"Want to tell me about it, Neil?" McGrady asked casually.

His eyes narrowed as he took a deep breath. "I had an investment deal go sour. Some illegal activity came to light, I pulled my investors out of it. A couple of fellows who lost their shirts have been making threats."

"Interesting."

"I think it's just hot air," he said in a not-very-convincing tone.

"Names?" McGrady picked up his notebook.

"Jake Delaney and Steven Woodword. I can't believe either of those fellows would be so stupid—"

"In my business, you're never surprised at the stupidity of people," he sighed. "Anybody in your life, Courtney, who might want to run you off the road?"

She shook her head and explained that she was new to Manitou and was spending the summer with a middle-aged aunt.

"Well, I guess there's nothing much to be done until we see what the officers find up there on the mountain. I'll look into alibis for these two suspects, and we'll go from there." He stood up. "In the meantime, Neil, I'd watch my back a little."

When he came back to the den after seeing McGrady to the door, Neil said, "I still think it was a random act. I'm not about to go around looking over my shoulder all the time."

"But what if it was one of those men?"

Neil saw the pallor on Courtney's face. "Hey, don't look like that. It's over. Let's make the best of the situation." He smiled as he added, "I hope you won't be in any hurry to leave. The Jacuzzi could do wonders for our battered bodies."

She flushed. *Minus a swimming suit?*

As if reading her thoughts, he said, "You'll find some extra swimming suits in the dressing room. Maribeth leaves some of her things here."

Courtney suspected he was lying. It wasn't only his sister who provided extra swimwear. Clearly, his bachelor pad was complete with all the amenities for entertaining.

"How about it? Nice, hot soothing water massaging every ache and pain? You'll love it."

Courtney knew she would. If every muscle in her body hadn't been aching from the strenuous climb up the mountainside, she might have declined. She'd never had an occasion to get into a fancy whirlpool tub, but it sounded heaven blessed.

The choice of a swimming suit was limited to several bikinis hanging in a small bathroom off the terrace swimming pool and Jacuzzi. The scanty pieces of cloth did little to hide the bruises and scratches on her lightly tanned body.

He was already in the Jacuzzi when she came out with a towel snugly tied around her. "Come on in. The temperature is wonderful."

As she hesitated, he could tell that she wasn't

used to this kind of experience, and his protective feelings surprised him. He made a pretense of looking at one of the jets while she dropped the towel and slipped into the water.

"Mmm," she purred, as the water massage began to do wonderful things to her aching muscles.

"Nice, huh?" Smiling, he stayed a discreet distance from her for a while. Leaning his head back against the tub's edge, he said, "When life gets a little bit too much, I just close my eyes and let the world float away."

"Sounds like a wonderful way to cope with things," she said with obvious envy. "I remember when I was a little girl, I had a little secondhand swimming pool. I used to spend hours in it. Then it sprung a leak, and my mother threw it away. She promised me a new one, but I never got it." Courtney sighed. "Funny how some disappointments stay with you."

"Yes, isn't it."

The thoughtful way he said it made her feel guilty. Here she was talking about the loss of a kiddie swimming pool, when he'd had to cope with the tragic death of someone he'd chosen to share his life. She wondered if he was as deeply lonely at heart as she was.

Impulsively, she moved closer to him in the water. He seemed a little surprised, but reached out and found her hand under the water. As the buoyancy of the water eliminated the distance between them, his hands slipped to the inviting span of her waist and she turned to him. Without hesitation, he drew her close.

The shared terrifying experience had bonded them in a strange way. His lips found hers, and they clung together until their physical contact changed from one of reassurance to one of demanding passionate desire.

His hands found the tie string on her halter, then he cupped the smooth, pliable softness of her breasts. As he kissed and caressed her, his legs moved purposefully in the water to capture hers. He knew that this lovemaking water ritual was new to her. As he began to lead her, he felt a flicker of guilt. She was literally out of her depth in this situation, and he knew it.

He gently pulled away, moving his lips to her forehead. They needed a time-out. If they ended up making love, he wanted to be damn sure there would be no regrets on her part.

"Now, it's time to relax with a drink," he said huskily. As he pulled away from her, she looked startled and questioning. How could he explain that there was no rejection of her in his behavior—just the opposite? She appealed to him in ways he wouldn't have thought possible, and he needed some assurance from her that she was ready for a sexual commitment.

"We need to talk," he said simply as he eased out of the tub.

Courtney watched Neil's glistening body move away in a strong, purposeful stride, and her chest tightened with an undefined ache. What had happened? Had she been too forward? Or not aggressive enough? Obviously, he'd found her wanting in some way.

She moved like someone in a state of limbo as she dressed again, and made her way to the den. Her mind searched for a way to escape the humiliation of what had occurred in the Jacuzzi. How could she pretend nothing had happened? A minute more and they would have been naked and clinging together. She'd never been filled with that kind of fiery desire.

He had changed into tan slacks and a matching cotton shirt. His damp hair fell in waves on his forehead as he smiled and held out a drink.

"Try my specialty."

She shook her head. "No, thanks. I think it's time I went and checked on my little one. I'll call a taxi."

"Not until we talk." He set the glass down with a punctuating bang.

She moved back as he tried to put his hands on her arms. "I don't think we have anything to talk about."

"Maybe you don't, but I do," he said firmly. "Something wonderful almost happened between us. You know it, and I know it."

"But why…?"

"Why did I stop? I wasn't about to take advantage of the situation. After what you've been through today, you might not be thinking straight. I wasn't sure that's what you really wanted." His voice thickened. "I'm aching to take you to bed, now, this moment."

His words released the heavy pain of rejection she'd been feeling. Her eyes were suddenly moist as she whispered, "Yes. Take me to bed."

They were halfway up the stairs to his bedroom when the doorbell stopped them.

"Damn," Neil swore.

"You'd better see who it is. McGrady may have come back with some news."

She lingered on the steps while Neil crossed the foyer and opened the front door to an attractive, fashionably dressed and very, very angry young woman.

"You low-down, lying scum," she lashed out in a wild tirade. "How could you just drop me cold like that? I thought everything was great between us." She accused him of deceit and demanded to know why he had led her to believe he cared for her.

"What are you talking about, Lisa? We had some good times, yes," he countered in an even tone. "That's all there was, and you know it. I never led you to believe anything else. We had that understanding from the very beginning."

"Maybe you did, but I didn't."

"You're trying to make some heartrending love affair out of a few dates. I'm sorry, Lisa, but you're way off base."

As Courtney listened to their raised voices, a cold question hit her like a chill. Was she about to allow herself to be drawn into the same kind of heartache as this woman? Neil had been honest with her from the beginning. Obviously, becoming sexually involved with him would be a momentary affair. Even as she asked herself if she was willing to settle for only that, she knew the answer. She wanted more for herself, and her child.

Neil closed the door as Lisa flung one last oath at him and stomped away. He turned toward the stairs and was surprised when Courtney came down to meet him.

"I'll call that taxi now," she said as she brushed by him.

"Wait a minute. You don't understand. Let me explain the situation."

"There's no need."

"I think there is." He reached for her.

"Don't!" She drew back. "Don't embarrass me any further. I want to leave."

"I get it. Don't confuse the situation with the truth, is that it?"

"Call me a taxi."

He reached into his pocket and pulled out some keys. "No need for a taxi. We can take my Jeep."

As they drove in silence to Maribeth's house, Neil cursed the timing of Lisa's emotional harangue. She'd dated him on the rebound in the first place, and when their relationship had petered off about three months ago, Neil suspected she'd gone back to her former sweetheart. Why she'd suddenly appeared, filled with revengeful fury, he didn't know, but she'd picked a hell of a time to do it.

Glancing at Courtney's rigid profile, he silently groaned. Total disaster. How could he explain that she stirred deep emotions that had lain dormant for a long time? He had slowed things down earlier because he wanted to respect her feelings—and look what happened!

"Courtney, please, let me—"

"No, don't...don't say anything. Just let it go, okay?" There was a finality in her tone that kept him from insisting.

When they picked up Jamie, Maribeth was full of

questions about the shooting, and Courtney was grateful that the conversation covered up the real reason for her emotional drain.

"Your aunt called a few minutes ago. I told her about the shooting, and assured her that both of you were okay. I guess she was wondering why the funeral had taken so long."

Courtney was puzzled and irritated. Was Devanna checking up on her by calling Maribeth? Was she thinking about picking up Jamie on her own?

After they left his sister's house, Neil did his best to try to breach the emotional chasm between them, but his efforts were in vain.

"I don't want to talk about it," Courtney said firmly as she told him goodbye at the door of the houseboat and went inside to face a stormy greeting from her aunt.

"Well, aren't you a sight! Clothes torn. Scratched and bruised. You don't look in any condition to take care of a baby."

"I'm banged up a little—but alive. Maribeth told you what happened?"

"Oh, she told me all right. She said the car stopped before it crashed at the bottom."

Courtney was surprised at her aunt's reaction. She must have been terribly worried when Maribeth told her about the shooting. Her face was flushed with anger and Courtney had never seen her so emotional. If the baby had been with them, her aunt probably would have had a heart attack by now.

"I'm fine, really I am," Courtney insisted. "And

Detective McGrady is optimistic about finding the shooter."

Devanna stared at her with a blank, unreadable stare. Without another word, she stomped to her room and slammed the door.

Chapter Six

She held Buzz's photo inches from her face and swore angrily, "I did what you said! Just the way you planned. Picked out the right spot. Waited until the car came around the curve. Fired and took out three tires."

Her eyes lit up with a fiery gloating. "You should have seen it, Buzz! The car skidded all over the road. Went up on two wheels and over the edge. I could hear it crashing down the mountain, but I had to get out of there quick. I waited a couple of hours and then called Maribeth to hear the sad news and pick up the baby."

She swore again. "The whole thing was for nothing. Just a few scratches, that's all. Now, I've got to do the whole thing again."

She stared at the photo as if listening. "No, she doesn't suspect anything. Keeps trying to make all sweet with me. She's convinced I'm her aunt, all right. That Neil fellow looks at me funny sometimes, but don't worry, everything's under control. You'll see. I've got a different plan."

COURTNEY WAS SURPRISED when Detective McGrady stopped by the next day to see her. "Just checking to see how you're feeling."

"I'm a little stiff and sore," she admitted. "But I'm not complaining. Won't you come in?" She turned to her aunt who was sitting on one of the counter stools. "Aunt Devanna, this is Detective McGrady."

Her aunt's expression wavered for a moment. Her eyes quickly took in his unassuming, good-old-boy appearance, then one of her rare smiles lifted the corners of her mouth. "My goodness, I'd never take you for a policeman."

"I get that quite a lot, ma'am." He smiled back, slightly twirling his hat in his hand. "I hope I'm not intruding, dropping by like this."

"Oh, not at all. Won't you sit down?" Devanna eagerly motioned toward the couch. "Can you tell us what you've learned about yesterday's horrible accident?"

"No accident, ma'am," McGrady corrected. "Someone took deliberate aim at the car." He turned to Courtney as she sat down beside him. "I was hoping you might have noticed a vehicle parked off the road somewhere close to that curve. Neil says he didn't see anything, but he was driving. Sometimes a passenger looking out the window will notice something."

She searched her memory. The only thing she recalled was how much she was enjoying the lovely mountain view when the horror began. Her stomach tightened as remembered terror assaulted her again.

"I'm sorry. If there was a car anywhere close, I didn't see it."

"The shooter had to have transportation. Knowing what kind might help." He patted her hand. "It's all right. If something comes to mind, let me know."

Devanna leaned forward in her chair. "Do you have any idea who did the shooting?"

"We have some suspects," he said as he massaged his chin in a thoughtful way.

"The men Neil told you about?" Courtney asked anxiously. "Delaney and Woodword?"

He nodded. "Neither of them have confirmed alibis. We have witnesses who overheard the men threatening to pay Neil back for sabotaging their real estate scheme."

"Thank goodness," breathed Courtney.

"Just talk, and not enough evidence for the D.A. to bring any kind of charges."

Courtney's chest tightened. "That means that Neil may still be in danger, doesn't it?"

"Could be," McGrady admitted regretfully.

Until that moment, Courtney hadn't realized the failed attempt might not be the end of the danger. Neil's life could still be in jeopardy every minute of every day. A hurricane of emotions suddenly assaulted her. All doubts about how she felt about him were swept away.

"You have to do something," she pleaded. "You have to keep him safe."

"We're moving as fast as we can on the investigation," McGrady assured her.

"Sounds to me like those men mean business," Devanna warned.

"We'll do our best to make sure your niece isn't put through that kind of trauma again," McGrady said. "Neil agrees with me."

"Looks like this Neil fellow has set himself up as a prize target," Devanna commented briskly. "If she keeps running around with him, no telling what might happen."

"It's true. Someone may want to get even with Neil through her." He turned to Courtney. "Might be a good idea to watch your back."

"Yes, she should be careful," Devanna agreed. Reaching over, she patted Courtney's hand. "We have to keep Jamie's mommy safe, don't we?"

"It's Neil who's in danger," Courtney insisted, drawing her hand away. "I want to help. What can I do?"

"Stay alert," McGrady answered readily. "If you remember something that doesn't add up, let me know. Sometimes the missing piece to a puzzle shows up where we least expect it."

"Isn't that the truth," Devanna agreed. "You just have to be open to suggestion. Sometimes the answer is right in front of you."

Courtney was in no mood to follow her aunt's meandering logic. The situation seemed clear enough. McGrady needed to find some hard evidence against the gunman who had tried to send her and Neil to their deaths.

"Maybe Neil should have a bodyguard."

McGrady chuckled. "I can't see a strong-minded guy like Neil taking to having a nursemaid, can you? We'll keep enough heat on Delaney and Woodword to make sure they don't try it again." He got up to take his leave. "Oh, by the way. The officers that checked out the wrecked car found your purse. I gave it to Neil and he said he would see that you got it."

A wave of relief swept over her.

After talking a few more minutes, McGrady took his leave, promising to keep them informed. Devanna seemed in an especially good mood after he left, but his visit had stirred up a myriad of emotions in Courtney.

"I'm going to take a walk," she told her aunt when the baby woke up. She needed to get away somewhere to think and come to terms with the churning inside her.

"Good idea. I'll watch the baby."

"He needs some fresh air. I'll use the baby backpack and take him with me."

"That's a stupid idea! Why do you want to jostle him around like that?"

Courtney closed her ears to Devanna's harangue about carrying Jamie around like some helpless papoose, and packed a bottle and a couple of diapers in the backpack.

"You'll just have yourself to blame if he gets sick."

She left the houseboat with a sigh of relief, and began walking in an easterly direction along the lake's edge. The day was warm, and she was glad she was wearing shorts and a comfortable blue summer top.

Carrying Jamie on her back wasn't as easy as

she'd thought, but she kept walking along the water's edge until she came to some smooth rocks reaching out over the water, and decided it was time to rest.

She saw a sprawling modern building a short distance away. Some kind of recreational club, she decided. From her position on the rocks, she was able to make out tennis courts, a swimming pool, and some small boats anchored at a dock. She was glad she'd stopped before she'd walked that far. Being around strangers was the last thing she needed at the moment.

Holding Jamie in her lap, she tried to react to the serene beauty of the moment, but her thoughts betrayed her. Was this the side of the lake where Jensen's body had been found?

As her mind pursued this unwelcome avenue, other unanswered questions puzzled her. Why had the gentle man's death and funeral been framed in violence? Had Jensen been in some way involved in Neil's investment deal that went sour? Could it be that his murder and the attempt on Neil's life were somehow connected? Courtney shivered even though the warmth of the noonday sun brought a shine of perspiration to her brow.

She carefully shaded Jamie from the direct sun. Cooing in good humor, he played with her finger and tried to put it in his slobbering mouth. Everything else in her life might be in shambles, but the one, undeniable blessing was her baby.

As she nuzzled his tummy and heard his chortled giggle, her spirits lightened. She had a family now. She wasn't alone any more. Her son made any challenge the world threw at her doable.

A few minutes later when she saw someone coming alone on the beach from the direction of the club, she felt an unreasonable annoyance at the invasion of her privacy.

It was a man, she could see that, and she mentally prepared herself to give him the cold shoulder if he tried to strike up a conversation.

As he approached, his gait seemed to quicken, and before she had time to prepare herself for recognition, he was almost upon her. She stared in disbelief as he waved his hand and gave her that disarming smile of his.

Neil!

"Hi, fancy meeting you here," he quipped as he dropped down beside her. "Yes, it's me. You know what they say about a bad penny?"

She could tell there was a questioning beneath his flippancy, as if he wasn't sure of her reaction to his sudden appearance. She wasn't sure about her response, either. Her heart had quickened upon seeing him again, but at the same time, a myriad of defenses had instantly fallen into place. The intimacy that had exploded between them was as much her fault as his, and she wasn't ready to invite that kind of emotional upheaval again.

"How did you find me?" She kept her tone level despite a sudden breathless feeling.

"My brilliant power of deduction," he answered facetiously, as if determined to keep the conversation light. "Your aunt said you were out for a walk with Jamie. I was pretty sure you'd head in this direction because it's easier walking. After driving to the Lakeside Recreation Center, I parked the car, and started back this way to find you. And here you are!" He searched her face. "It's all right, isn't it?"

"Yes." What else could she say?

"I just had to see you. There are things I need to get off my chest."

She shook her head. "Not now."

"We have to talk sometime," he insisted. "What am I going to do with all these rehearsed speeches in my mind if you never let me say them?" He gave her one of his disarming smiles. "That's cruel and unjust punishment, you know. Condemning a man without a hearing will weigh on your conscience. We don't want that, do we?" he asked as he dramatically put his hand over his heart.

"Oh, stop it," she said, laughing in spite of herself. His antics had a strange way of mocking the importance she had given the whole embarrassing incident. "All right, I'll let you have your say, but not now. I just want to enjoy the fresh air, warm sun, and beautiful view."

"I'll go along with that," he agreed, and a tight chord in his chest began to relax. It was going to be all right, he thought. The first hurdle was over. She hadn't slapped his face and walked away.

For the next hour, they were able to step outside all unwelcome pressures as they talked, laughed, and put a different frame around their being together. They both skirted away from discussing the questions that weighed heavily on them.

"What do you say to lunch at the rec center?" Neil offered. "Nothing fancy. Everybody's running around in exercise clothes, and being themselves."

Just the thought of going back to the suffocating
atmosphere of the houseboat made it easy for Courtney to accept the invitation. She was determined to
enjoy Neil's company as she would have a pleasant
companion's. It wasn't his fault she'd almost gone
over the deep end about him. There'd be no need to
avoid him if she could keep her head on straight. His
past romantic affairs were none of her business—and
she intended to keep it that way. All she wanted was
his safety, and an end to any threats against him.

Neil insisted on carrying Jamie in the backpack
as they walked to the recreation center. More than
one pair of eyes widened as they flickered over the
baby and then settled speculatively on Courtney as
if thinking, *Neil's latest conquest?*

No doubt, there'd be a bevy of rumors flying
around in short order, Courtney thought. But then decided she didn't care.

Her total unconcern about the gossip surprised
her. As it turned out, she found herself at the center
of attention for another reason. Many of Neil's ac-
quaintances had heard, or read about, the shooting
incident, and the two of them were hit with a barrage
of questions.

"Is she the one who was with you?"

"Have they found the gunman?"

"Why was someone shooting at the two of you?"

Neil deftly fielded all the questions as best he
could until they could escape to a private dining
room where he had a membership.

During lunch, Neil tried several avenues of conversation without much success. The world had

swept back on them, and destroyed the cocoon they'd briefly been able to put around themselves.

"Let me show you around," he suggested after they'd eaten.

She shook her head. "I should be getting back."

"Why?"

She didn't have an answer. She'd changed Jamie, given him his bottle, and he had fallen asleep in her arms.

"There's lots of activity going on in the center. You might see something that appeals to you. Are you a tennis player?"

She shook her head.

"How about Ping-Pong?"

As they passed a room filled with pool tables, she smiled.

"Don't tell me." Neil laughed in honest surprise. "Pool? You play pool?"

Courtney started to deny it, but a kaleidoscope of memories challenged her honesty. "My father's occupation as a transient welder kept him on the move. The one constant in his life was his membership in a Brotherhood Lodge, and there was usually a local chapter wherever his job took him. While he spent time in the bar, or playing poker, and Mom was busy with the women's auxiliary, I was free to hang out in the game room, watching the pool players."

"And you did more than watch," Neil prompted with a twinkle in his eye.

She nodded. From the time she was tall enough to look over the edge of the pool table, she had managed to have a pool cue in her hands as often as possible. But when she reached adolescence, she realized that her prowess at the pool table was not an acceptable achievement for a young woman who desperately needed friends her age. She'd never admitted to her late husband that she'd ever been near a pool table.

The way Neil was looking at her made her toss her head. "Would you like to have me prove it to you?"

"By all means." He loved the way her eyes were sparkling with defiance. He couldn't believe that this totally feminine woman was going to challenge him to a game of pool. Should he warn her that he never held back or feigned a loss?

She hesitated. "What about the baby?"

Was she going to use Jamie as an excuse to back out of the challenge? He'd hoped to enjoy a side of her he'd never glimpsed before. He felt a pang of disappointment.

"How about we make a bed out of a couple of chairs," he suggested. "And let Jamie sleep while his mother proves herself?"

"Fine." She smiled at his eagerness. "Is eight ball okay?"

Fortunately one of the pool tables was free. Courtney selected a cue stick from the wall rack, and Neil could tell from the way she handled and chalked it that he might be in for more of a challenge than he expected.

"I'll rack 'em and you break," she offered.

"No, ladies first," he said. He'd been no slouch about picking up some extra money at pool halls when he was in college.

As she deftly broke, the nine ball went into a corner pocket. "Okay, I'm shooting stripes, you're solids."

Graceful, intent, she moved around the table, eyeing her shots. Her supple body created a beautiful vision of concentration as she repeatedly pocketed ball after ball. Neil was mesmerized by the control she had over the game, and he realized allowing her to break had been an acknowledgment of her feminine inferiority, which was proving to be way off base. She ran the table, and took him for a second game more decisive than the first.

"I concede." Neil put his arm around her waist and laughed. "A pool shark, if I ever met one."

Courtney's face flushed with pleasure. She couldn't remember when she'd felt so fully alive. The way Neil was looking at her made her victory worth more than a silver trophy.

"I claim the right of a rematch," he teased.

"Anytime," she said with a confident toss of her fair head.

Neil gently picked up Jamie and settled him in his arms. "If you've had enough exercise, I'll drive the two of you back."

She knew her high spirits would instantly take a dive once she returned to the houseboat, but she really had no choice but to accept the offer.

"By the way, I have your purse in the car. I assured McGrady that I would personally deliver it."

As they left the building and were heading for Neil's car in the parking lot, he came to an abrupt stop.

The man coming toward them was Jake Delaney.

His face turned an ugly purple when he saw Neil. His eyes bulged and he looked ready to explode.

"You bastard!" He hunched up his thick shoulders like a bull ready to paw the ground.

"Watch it, Delaney," Neil ordered sharply as he quickly handed the baby to Courtney and stepped in front of her.

"Setting the cops on me, did you? Accusing me of shooting up your car?" He waved his clenched fists. "I ought to knock you sideways. Give you something to howl about."

"I didn't accuse you of anything. I just told the detective about the bad feelings between us over the investment deal."

"Pointing your damn finger at me, that's what you were doing."

"The police asked me who might be angry enough to send my car off a cliff, and after our last telephone conversation, you came to mind."

"Hell, when I get even with you, I'll make damn sure I don't miss."

"Careful, Delaney. Is that another one of your threats?"

"More like a promise." His angry glare swept over Courtney. "You've taken up with bad company, lady. I'd put a wide berth between you and Neil Ellsworth, if I were you."

"She doesn't need any advice coming from a guy who has had one foot outside the law all his life."

"I'm just warning her that hanging around you might not be the best thing for her health. No telling what might happen—"

Neil lunged forward. He caught the man's chin in an uppercut. The blow sent Delaney sprawling backward onto his butt.

"Get up," Neil ordered, standing over him. "Repeat that threat, and I'll knock a few teeth down your throat."

Delaney wiped the blood trickling out the corner of his mouth. "By God, you'll pay for that."

Neil was ready when Delaney got to his feet, but instead of coming at Neil, he stomped away. When he was almost to the door of the building, he turned, shook his fist and shouted a volley of cuss words.

"Let's get out of here." Neil took Courtney's arm.

His thunderous expression was like a storm about to break and the ugly scene had ignited all of Courtney's fears over Neil's safety.

Neither of them spoke until they were back at the houseboat. She was glad Devanna's gray van was gone. She was not up to dealing with her aunt's eccentricities.

Neil accompanied Courtney inside, and waited until she'd settled Jamie with a bottle in his bassinet before he took her hand and pulled her down on the couch beside him. The lovely mood between them had been completely shattered by the ugly encounter with Delaney.

"Do you think he's the one who shot at us?" Courtney asked anxiously.

"I don't know," Neil admitted. "I've always thought Delaney more talk than anything, but he does have a record. He spent a few years in the pen for embezzlement. If he is the shooter, I bet Woodword put him up to it. He's more of a manipulator than Delaney, and was the idea man behind this last scam."

"You'll have to tell McGrady. Get a restraining order against them, or something?"

"I'm afraid a piece of paper isn't going to help much." He touched her anxious face, letting his fingers smooth the worry lines around eyes. "But as wonderful as it was to be with you today, I'm not going to expose you to any more danger. Until this is settled, one way or another, the only safe thing to do is keep a distance between us."

"I'm not afraid."

"You should be." He gave her a wry smile. "I won't be pestering you for any more dates. I'm not taking any more chances."

"It's you I'm worried about." She shivered, remembering the venom in Delaney's eyes.

He drew her close and lowered his mouth to hers.

As she clung to him, his kisses were long, tender and passionate, but there was a finality about them that brought tears to Courtney's eyes.

When he set her away from him, he got up and left the houseboat without another word.

"Stay safe," she whispered. She didn't know why an insidious premonition warned her that the decision he had made to stay away from her was somehow terribly wrong.

Chapter Seven

Courtney sensed a subtle change in her aunt's attitude toward her. Devanna began asking questions about Neil as if she were suddenly interested in how serious their relationship might be.

"I suppose he'll be hanging around," she said, a questioning lift in her voice.

"Maybe not," Courtney sighed and told Devanna about the confrontation with Delaney the day before.

Her aunt's eyes glittered with interest. "And this guy made a threat against you?"

Courtney nodded. She'd never forget Delaney's fiery eyes burning into hers. "He warned me to stay away from Neil."

"He did, did he?"

Courtney took a deep breath. "And Neil took him seriously."

"Well, I would say so." Devanna nodded emphatically, as if her thoughts were whirling in some unknown direction. Her tone was speculative. "You might be in all kinds of danger."

"It's Neil I'm worried about," Courtney answered shortly.

"Oh, things are like that, are they?"

"I don't know what you mean," Courtney lied. She wasn't about to admit she lay awake at night, reliving the memory of his kisses and caresses. "There's nothing serious between us."

"Well, I can't say that I'm surprised," her aunt said with brutal frankness. "He walks around like he could buy just about anything…or anybody."

"He does not," Courtney said, flaring.

"You've got moondust in your eyes. You don't want to see things the way they really are," she scoffed. "Stuck-up people like that stick in my craw. Treat you like dirt under their feet. They'd just as soon kick you into the gutter as look at you."

"Neil's not like that!"

"We'll see," Devanna answered in a prophetic tone, as if she were privy to some special insight. "Maybe he'll come around again, and maybe he won't. Anyway, you're a lot better off staying away from him. Stuck-up people with money are bad news."

Courtney choked back a building fury. How dare her aunt make such judgmental pronouncements? Hadn't she married a man with money? The more she got to know Devanna, the less she understood her. It was becoming harder and harder to keep her mouth shut.

Courtney was glad when her aunt suddenly seemed too preoccupied with other things to spend much time with her or Jamie. She was away from the

houseboat a lot, and, for the first time since Courtney's arrival, she came back, weary from shopping.
Her arms were full of packages, and almost everything she'd bought was for the baby.

"Look at this. I just couldn't resist it," she exclaimed, holding up a miniature sailor's outfit with
matching booties. "And this…and this." Sleepers,
blankets, bibs and a half-dozen new outfits.

Courtney was speechless. She'd been very frugal
when she bought a layette and baby clothes, and
washing had been a daily routine. She looked in disbelief at the pile of Devanna's purchases.

"I bought a larger size in some things. That way
he'll grow into them," she said proudly. "I can hardly
wait to see how darling he looks in them."

Courtney wanted to protest that it would be mid-
winter before Jamie would be big enough for some
of the new outfits. Surely Devanna wasn't thinking
she and the baby were going to live somewhere else
with her when summer was over? The thought of living year round with her eccentric aunt was enough
to curdle her stomach. The few weeks she'd spent on
the houseboat had been less than comfortable. If it
hadn't been for Neil, they would have been close to
unbearable, and she'd already begun to make plans
for an earlier departure than originally planned.

"You must have spent a bundle on all of this,"
Courtney said.

"Our darling little boy is worth it."

Courtney couldn't figure out why her aunt was suddenly willing to spend money. She'd always been
miserly about sharing the cost of groceries and ne-

cessities, making sure that Courtney paid her share or more. Now, the way she was suddenly spending money was a total shock. Courtney couldn't figure it out.

Devanna replaced a lot of the baby's bottles, nipples and other paraphernalia. She came back from her shopping trips carrying purchases that she took directly to her room. When the door was left open, Courtney could see boxes and sacks piled up on the top bunk.

When Courtney asked her about extra food supplies she was buying, Devanna just shrugged. "It doesn't hurt to be prepared."

For what? Courtney was more puzzled than ever, but decided if Devanna had caught a shopping bug, there wasn't any harm in it. Her mood was definitely improved.

She even invited Courtney to go shopping with her. "You could point out some more of the things the baby might be needing."

"I can't think of another thing," Courtney answered honestly. "And I'm not much of a shopper."

"I bought a couple of books about feeding him solid food, and all." She hesitated. "I thought we might look through them together."

Courtney doubted that she'd heard correctly. Was her aunt really reaching out to her. This offer to spend companionable time together took her completely by surprise.

"I'd like that," she answered quickly. Maybe the kind of relationship she'd hoped for was going to develop between them after all. Her spirits lifted as the two of them sat down together and went through some of the books.

There were other changes in her aunt, too. She'd never been interested in sharing any of the cooking. More often than not, she fixed something for herself, or brought back something from a fast-food restaurant. She'd never made an effort to eat with Courtney.

"How about I bring home some carryout for supper for us?" she asked as she prepared to leave on one of her shopping trips.

Startled, Courtney responded, "Sounds good. Thank you."

"There's a good seafood place that has wonderful food. How about that?"

"Perfect."

"Good, I'll get some clam chowder and a couple of combo plates."

Devanna's sudden willingness to provide a meal for both of them bordered on the miraculous. Courtney couldn't get over the change in her behavior. Even though Devanna's possessiveness over Jamie was hard to take sometimes, Courtney couldn't fault the obvious love she had for the baby.

While Courtney waited for her aunt to return, she spent the afternoon sitting on the deck with Jamie in his carrier. Restless, and unable to put Neil out of her mind, her eyes kept traveling across the lake, searching for a sign of his boat.

Her hope that he might have relented and would come to see her faded as the afternoon ended. There was a tightness in her chest as she tried to reassure herself that the shooter would not try to harm him again with the police alerted to the situation.

When Devanna returned, she had a new rattle for Jamie and two dinners from one of Manitou's popular restaurants.

Courtney set the table, and Devanna dished out steaming bowls of chowder while Jamie played on a blanket with his new rattle.

"Plenty of clams and potatoes, that's what I like," Devanna said as she set the bowls on the counter. "And warm cornbread."

As she reached for a piece, her elbow hit her water glass and tipped it right into her lap. She squealed, jumped up, and swore, "Damn it all!"

Drenched from the waist down, she started toward her bedroom. "Go ahead and eat. I'll change and be right back."

The aroma of the thick chowder had already stimulated Courtney's taste buds, and she wasn't about to argue. She dipped her spoon into the chowder, and had taken only a small sip when Jamie let out a howl.

"It's all right, darling."

He'd hit himself in the forehead with his new rattle, and she tried not to laugh at his surprised expression. As she bent down to pick up him, a fierce burning hit her in the pit of her stomach.

She groaned, nearly doubling over.

Leaving Jamie on the blanket, she covered her mouth with her hand and dashed to the bathroom. Groaning, she dropped to the floor in front of the toilet. Heaving and violently sick, weak and dizzy, she rid her stomach of the small amount of soup she'd consumed.

She wavered to her feet a few minutes later. A paralyzing weakness threatened her whole body as she stumbled out the bathroom door. Devanna stood there looking at her and holding the baby.

"The soup," Courtney croaked. "It's bad."

"Oh, my God," Devanna swore. "Are you sure?"

Courtney didn't have the strength to answer. She barely made it to the lower bunk in her room and collapsed on it. Doubling up, she groaned and writhed, praying that the misery in her body would soon pass.

Thank God, Devanna was there to take care of Jamie, she thought, as her aunt hovered in the doorway, watching.

Courtney had never given a thought to what would happen to Jamie if she wasn't around to take care of him. The near fatal shooting, and now food poisoning, brought home a frightening reality. There was no one on her side of the family but Devanna to take over the care of her son. He would be in good hands, she thought as the pain slowly subsided, and she finally fell into an exhausted sleep.

Her escape was short-lived. In the middle of the night, the painful trauma gave rise to a terrifying nightmare. She fled along the water's edge with Jamie in her arms. Someone was at her heels, ready to snatch the baby from her—but she couldn't see who it was. Hot breath seared the back of her neck, and a ghoulish cry filled her ears as she clutched the baby against her heaving breast. Suddenly she tripped and fell. A vague, threatening figure snatched

Jamie out of her arms and disappeared into the fog-laced darkness.

Courtney cried aloud as she jerked awake and sat up with her heart pounding. The threat of losing the baby was so real that every muscle in her body tensed and perspiration beaded on her forehead. A mocking stillness was broken only by the never-ending lapping of water against the sides of the houseboat.

Jamie! Where was Jamie?

Then she remembered. The baby was safely in Devanna's care. Apparently her cry had not awakened him or her aunt. She could see that the bassinet was gone, and decided her aunt had wisely taken it into her room for the night.

Toward early morning when she got up to go to the bathroom, she saw that Devanna's door was still closed. Although still weak and shaky, her body had thankfully recovered from the small intake of the bad soup, and she made her way to the galley to fix herself some tea and toast.

She was surprised how clean everything was. The counter had been cleared, the sink emptied of dishes, and no sign of the treacherous clam chowder. Courtney shivered as she thought about what might have happened if she and her aunt had eaten the entire order. If Devanna hadn't spilled the water, and Jamie hadn't hit himself with the rattle, they both could be in the hospital with food poisoning.

She was stretched out of on the sofa when Devanna came in with the baby. A look of total surprise crossed her aunt's face.

"I thought…you'd be…" Devanna stammered.

"Me, too," Courtney admitted. "I still feel a little woozy, but I was lucky. We both were, considering how close we both came to getting deathly ill on the tainted soup."

Devanna didn't respond as she fixed Jamie's bottle and sat down to feed him. Courtney knew she should probably take over with the baby, but she felt totally depleted.

Her aunt's scowling expression clearly showed she was out of sorts about something. Resting her heavy head on one hand, Courtney asked, "Did Jamie keep you up? I'm sorry. I didn't hear him fussing."

Devanna made some noncommittal response, and Courtney had the impression that she was blaming her for getting sick. Irritated, Courtney said, "The clams in the chowder must have been bad, and gave me food poisoning."

"Yes, the clams," Devanna agreed.

"You should go back to that restaurant and complain."

"I dumped all of it down the sink," Devanna answered with obvious satisfaction. "No need to make a big fuss."

Courtney didn't bother to answer. She'd given up trying to follow the tangled mesh of her aunt's thinking.

THAT MORNING WHEN Neil arrived at his office, he was surprised to find McGrady already there, interviewing the staff, one by one.

"Just plowing a little ground," the detective explained. "You can never tell what a little spadework may dig up."

"Feel free to dig away," Neil said with a wave of his hand. "I haven't been able to come up with anything that might connect Jensen's murder with the attempt on my life. He was an accountant, not an investor."

"Are you sure?" McGrady asked lazily. "We've discovered Harold Jensen had quite a bit of money tucked away. We're looking into the possibility that he might have been a silent investor in some of Delaney and Woodword's financial schemes."

Neil's eyes widened. "I can't believe Jensen would keep something like that to himself. We had an honest relationship between us."

McGrady leaned back in a chair and frowned as he stared into space. "There's something here that I'm missing," he mused. "I can't get over a gut feeling that there's a connection between Jensen's shooting and yours."

"What on earth would that be?"

"I'm not sure. The only common denominator seemed to be your company."

When Neil told McGrady about his run-in with Jake Delaney, the detective wasn't pleased.

"We don't need an assault-and-battering charge messing up things. I reckon you'd better be holding on to that temper of yours."

"I couldn't help myself. His threats against me didn't mean anything, but when he leveled them at Courtney, I blew." Neil's face flushed with anger just thinking about it. "She's already been through enough. I decided to put some distance between us just to make sure she's not an innocent victim again."

"Sounds like a good idea," McGrady agreed. "You need to watch your backside pretty close. Until we get something solid, better to err on the side of caution and stay away from her."

"It's not going to be easy," Neil admitted.

"Seems like a nice lady," McGrady commented with a knowing smile as he got to his feet. "Well, I'll be moving along."

"Will you keep me posted if there are any new developments?"

"Don't hold your breath. There are a lot of loose ends, and I have a feeling nothing's going to change much."

He was wrong.

Later that afternoon, he called Neil with good news. A ripple of excitement coated every word. "The D.A. just announced that Delaney and Woodword have been arrested."

"For the shooting?"

"No, for another illegal scam that came to light when the authorities were looking into their affairs. They found enough evidence for an indictment of fraud."

Neil could hardly contain himself as he thanked the detective and hung up. Their arrest changed everything. Now Delaney's threats against Courtney were null and void.

By afternoon, Courtney felt she was once more among the living and, over Devanna's protests, she took charge of Jamie again.

"Jealous, that's what you are!" Giving a toss of her unnaturally red head, her aunt flounced out of the houseboat.

Courtney sighed as she heard her drive away. The harmony between them hadn't lasted very long. They seemed to be back to square one in their relationship.

"Jamie, love," Courtney cooed to the baby, "I think we both need some sun and fresh air."

She took him out on the deck, and set his carrier down beside her chair and shaded his face. He quickly drifted off for his afternoon nap. She leaned her head back against the chair and closed her eyes. Exhausted from the night's ordeal, and soothed by the warmth of the sun, she fell asleep.

The sound of a motorboat pulling into the dock woke her. Neil! Her first thought was one of joy, quickly followed by instant embarrassment. That morning she'd thrown on a faded pair of shorts, a baggy pullover, and had only given her hair a few perfunctory strokes.

"Oh, no! I look awful." She braced herself to greet him as he anchored the boat, and came quickly around the deck to where she was sitting.

In contrast to her unkempt appearance, his crisp white slacks were neatly creased. A dark blue knitted pullover stretched across his chest, and his jaunty captain's hat sat on the back of his head.

"What a surprise," she said, trying her best to put some enthusiasm into the greeting.

His smile faded. "My God, what's happened to you?"

Her complexion was a pasty yellow, her eyes heavy, and her lovely body slumped and lifeless as she sat there staring up at him.

"I...I've been sick," she stammered. "But I'm fine now."

"Sick? How? What?"

He pulled up a chair and reached for her hands. They felt cold as they clutched his. As he listened to her story, he was filled with a combination of relief and anger—relief because the food poisoning was a temporary condition, and anger because she'd been subjected to it at all.

When Courtney told him the name of the restaurant, he was surprised because it was one of Manitou's most popular and reliable eating places.

"Did you see a doctor?"

She shook her head. "I wasn't that sick. I mean, I got over it pretty fast."

He raised an eyebrow. "Yeah, I can see that. You're a bundle of energy. Ready to take me on in another game of pool."

"Well, maybe, not today," she admitted with a sheepish smile. "But I'm glad you came by. I'm surprised, though. The last time we talked, you had decided to put some distance between us."

"That's why I'm here. I have some good news. Delaney and Woodword have been arrested."

"For shooting at us?"

He shook his head. "No, for an illegal scam the

authorities discovered as they looked into their affairs. They moved quickly to arrest them before they could get out of the country."

"What a relief." She felt tears swelling up in her eyes. *Now Neil was safe.*

"They haven't admitted the vendetta against me, yet, but I'm sure they will. They have a pattern of violence." Then he smiled at Courtney. "You know what this means? Lucky me, I'm free to hang around now as much as you'll let me."

Just being in his company was like a shower of light breaking through a dark cloud. How could she resist the warmth he brought into her dull life?

"I think that can be arranged," she answered with mock solemnity.

He lifted one of her hands and brushed it with his lips. "I have to be out of town this week on business, but I'll see you as soon as I get back."

"I'll miss you."

He cupped her face with his hands as he kissed her, and murmured, "Me, too."

As he turned to leave, a flicker of a shadow across the floor of the deck caught his eyes. Moving quickly around the corner of the houseboat, he came face-to-face with Devanna. Even though he knew she'd been standing there listening, he repeated what he'd just told Courtney.

"I'm going to be gone a few days, but I'll check on her as soon as I get back."

"Don't worry, I'll take good care of her."

It was only later that he realized how her smile had been a mockery of the promise.

Chapter Eight

The next few days crept by at a snail's pace. Courtney still wasn't back to normal after the food poisoning, and she didn't feel like doing much of anything.
She slept, took care of Jamie, read a little and spent
time sunning on the deck.

In sharp contrast, her aunt was the epitome of energy, bustling about in the houseboat, or coming and
going in the van. She was obviously preoccupied,
and only responded vaguely to Courtney's occa-
sional attempts at conversation.

"I have things to do."

"If you wait until I feel better, I'll help."

"Don't need your help."

Devanna kept the small under-the-counter clothes
washer and dryer going most of the day, washing an
assortment of clothes Courtney had never seen her
wear. Why the burst of energy, Courtney wondered.

She began marking off the days until Neil would
return from his business trip. She knew she might be
setting herself up for a fall if she became dependent
upon his attention. For some reason he seemed taken

with her and the baby at the moment, but who knew how long that would last.

She was totally surprised and pleased when his sister, Maribeth, came by midweek, and invited her and Jamie to a small luncheon gathering at her house the next afternoon.

Courtney readily accepted the invitation. Escaping a few hours from the gloomy houseboat, and her aunt's indifferent company, would be a godsend.

"I'd love to come. How nice of you to ask me."

"There'll only be six of us. Nothing fancy," Maribeth assured her.

When Courtney told her aunt about the luncheon, Devanna didn't react in her usual negative way. In fact, she appeared to be glad Courtney was going to be gone from the houseboat for the afternoon.

"Enjoy yourself," she said with unusual graciousness. "Be sure and put one of those new jumper suits on Jamie. We don't want him wearing those faded, secondhand things you brought with you."

She eyed Courtney's short print skirt and white, off-the-shoulder blouse in a way that made Courtney feel her aunt included them in the secondhand category, as well.

Her enthusiasm for the outing began to fade. By the time she and the baby arrived at Maribeth's house, and she parked her old car alongside several new ones, she was feeling uncomfortable about being there.

She wondered if Neil had twisted his sister's arm to invite her, and she eyed the beautiful home and its decorative landscaping with misgivings. She didn't belong in these affluent gatherings and wondered what on earth had made her accept the invitation.

"Come in, come in," Maribeth greeted her with her usual bubbly warmth. "Everyone's in the family room. When Jamie gets tired of everyone making a fuss over him, Hazel can take him up to the nursery."

Maybe I can escape up there, too, Courtney thought, remembering how she hid out in the nursery once before. Maribeth was wearing a slenderizing white sharkskin pantsuit Courtney was certain hadn't come off a bargain rack.

As she passed the den, she remembered Neil's angry telephone conversation, and breathed a prayer of thankfulness that Delaney was safely behind bars.

The family room was almost as large Courtney's utilitarian apartment had been. Myriad windows gave a panoramic view of the surrounding mountains, and white and lemon-yellow furnishings lent splashes of color to leather furniture and maple-paneled walls.

Maribeth's guests lounged about on the leather furniture, drinking wine coolers out of tall, misty glasses. She was surprised when Peggy and Hollie greeted her warmly.

"Hi, Courtney."

"Nice to see you."

Remembering their friendliness at their husbands' birthday party, she was grateful Maribeth had included them at the luncheon. Maybe it was going to be a pleasant afternoon, after all.

"Let me hold the baby," Peggy begged, and took Jamie on her lap, cooing and tickling his tummy.

Maribeth quickly introduced her other two guests: Stella Penrose, a poised woman in her late forties, and her daughter, Pamela, a very attractive blonde wearing a silk dress that enhanced every curve in her slender body.

"It's very nice to meet you, Courtney," Stella responded in the polished manner of someone who knew her way around socially. "I understand you're spending the summer in Manitou."

"Yes, with my aunt," Courtney answered evenly, hoping to put an end to that avenue of conversation. A discussion of life aboard a houseboat was not a topic she wanted to invite.

The way Pamela Penrose's appraising eyes were taking inventory of her gave Courtney the feeling she'd been the topic of conversation before her arrival.

When Maribeth offered her wine or iced tea from a refreshment cart, Courtney readily chose tea.

"Try these appetizers," Peggy offered as Courtney sat down on the sofa beside her.

The conversation revolved around some upcoming social events involving all the women, and Courtney enjoyed a few minutes of relaxation. Too soon, her sense of well-being ended when Stella pulled her back into the limelight.

"Maribeth was telling us about Neil's and your horrible experience. I can't imagine such a thing happening," Stella said, frowning.

"I'm so glad they have the men in jail," Maribeth said with a sigh of relief.

"You must have been terrified, Courtney," Peggy

said, shivering. "I can't even imagine such an awful thing happening. It's too scary to even think about."

"Neil said she was absolutely wonderful," Maribeth bragged. "Even when it looked as if the car was going to go over the cliff any second, she didn't lose her head."

"Really?" Pamela's tone suggested skepticism.

Courtney was totally uncomfortable being the center of attention, and was relieved when Hazel appeared to take Jamie upstairs. Since they'd already met, Courtney was at ease handing the baby over to her.

"Well, now, I guess it's time for lunch," Maribeth said. "The table is set on the patio." She motioned toward a pair of French doors that led out of the family room to a brick patio.

Hollie fell into step beside Courtney, and asked in a low voice, "Are you feeling all right?"

"Fine," she reassured her.

"You look a little peaked."

"Just a little tired." Courtney decided Neil must not have told Maribeth about the food poisoning, or his sister would have surely asked her about it.

The table conversation at lunch flowed easily. As Maribeth and her other guests gossiped and shared plans for travel or upcoming events, Courtney was able to relax and enjoy the pleasure of being outside in the fresh air, bright sunshine and beautiful green lawn.

Still a little cautious about what she ate and drank, Courtney sipped her iced tea and gingerly picked at a salad made of avocado, seasoned artichoke and sliced turkey. Ordinarily, Courtney was a good eater, enjoying all kinds of food, but the lingering memory of how horribly sick she'd been kept her from eating with her usual appetite.

Maribeth did her best to include Courtney in the conversation, but without much success. The only common tie they all had was Neil.

"My brother tells me you beat the socks off of him at pool the other day," Maribeth said, chuckling. "I'd like to have seen that. Neil said you're a real champion. Even won a trophy or two, I hear."

An instant weighted silence engulfed the luncheon table as all the other women stared at her.

"You're a pool shark?" Hollie asked with open astonishment.

"Well, I'll be," Peggy laughed. "You don't look like the kind of gal who knows her way around a pool hall."

Courtney wanted to shrink up and fade away.

Stella Penrose looked at her with a disapproving downturn of her lips. "I can't imagine anyone spending time in those smoky, horrid places."

"Me, either," Pamela said with a slight quiver of her narrow nostrils.

"Well, I think it's great when a gal can beat a fellow at his own game," Maribeth said defensively, trying to defend her remarks that had put Courtney in a bad light.

"Didn't they have tennis courts where you grew up, Courtney?" Pamela asked with a slight smile. "I mean, playing pool is so…so?" She shrugged as if she couldn't find the right word to describe it.

"What about golf?" Stella asked as if she were doing her best to find some accomplishment that would make Courtney slightly more respectable. "The country club has some beautiful greens, and there's a ladies tournament every year that's great fun."

"I've tried other sports," Courtney replied evenly. "But I like pool the best."

Stella shrugged as if she'd done her best.

"Well, I'm glad you took my brother down a peg or two," Maribeth said, showing that she was on Courtney's side.

Stella cleared her throat. "I don't know if I should bring this up, Maribeth, but I saw that woman whom Neil used to date. You know, the divorcée. What was her name? Rosemary something? What ever happened with her and Neil?"

"They broke up," Maribeth answered shortly.

"For a while there, I thought Neil was headed for the altar for sure," Peggy commented.

"Not me." Hollie shook her head. "He's made it pretty clear he's going to be a perennial bachelor." Then she looked at Courtney and flushed.

"Well, I don't know what Neil Ellsworth is looking for in a woman," Pamela said tartly. "He wines and dines a gal, makes her believe he's serious about a commitment, and then poof, he's off to newer pastures." The look she exchanged with her mother spoke volumes to Courtney.

Pamela had been another one of Neil's conquests.

Courtney kept a smile on her face, but the conversation had brought home a truth that hit her like a cold slap to the face. *Wake up!* Neil's record spoke loud and clear. It wouldn't be very long before these same women would be talking about her. *It was doubtful his attention would even last till the end of the summer.*

"Would you like to help on the Labor Day Gala, Courtney?" Maribeth asked, valiantly trying to change the direction of the conversation.

"Oh, I won't be here," she heard herself saying. "Actually, I've decided it's about time for me to leave Manitou."

"I thought you were here for the summer. I mean, that's the impression I got from Neil."

"My plans have changed."

"Where will you go?"

"Back to Cheyenne, Wyoming. That's where my job is."

Verbalizing her departure brought a strange sense of release. Leaving was the only sensible decision. Her high hopes for a happy summer had been dashed almost from the first moment she'd arrived. She knew Devanna would make a fuss when she told her she was leaving, but only because of her affection for the baby. It was obvious that Devanna couldn't care less about whether she, Courtney, stayed or left.

After lunch, as soon as it was politely acceptable, Courtney thanked Maribeth for her hospitality and got ready to leave.

"If I don't see you again," Courtney told her, "I want you to know how much I've appreciated your friendship."

Maribeth hugged her. "If you change your mind, let me know, and we'll get together again."

Courtney promised, but already her decision to leave was firmly fixed her mind. As she drove back to the houseboat, she wondered when the best time would be to tell her aunt.

NEIL CALLED MARIBETH that evening from his Seattle hotel. He was anxious to know how the afternoon get-together had gone. He had persuaded his sister to give the luncheon especially for Courtney's benefit. It worried him that she looked so wan, and he thought it would do her good to get out and be with some other women.

"I'm not sure how it went," Maribeth answered honestly.

"What do you mean?"

"Courtney didn't look all that well. Only picked at her food."

"I told you she'd had a bout with food poisoning recently, so that doesn't surprise me."

"I'm afraid that Pamela and her mother made it a little uncomfortable for her—"

"You invited them?" Neil swore under his breath. He had dated Pamela a few times and knew firsthand how critical she and her mother could be. He'd given both of them a wide berth, and often wondered why on earth his sister continued to associate with them. "What on earth were you thinking?"

"I couldn't help it," Maribeth said regretfully. "They were sitting with Peggy and Hollie at the club when I asked them to the luncheon, and there wasn't anything I could do but include Stella and Pamela, too." She sighed. "It was a mistake."

"I could have told you that!"

When she told him about the pool fiasco, and the conversation about him and Rosemary, he groaned. He wouldn't have willingly put Courtney through that kind of social torture for anything in the world.

"I'm sorry, Neil," Maribeth said contritely. "I like Courtney, and I'm sorry to see her go. I wonder if she's up to traveling. It can't be easy with a baby—"

"What are you talking about?"

"Oh, didn't you know? She's leaving, going back to Wyoming."

Neil tightened his grip on the telephone. "What? When?"

"In the next few days, I guess, because she said she wouldn't be seeing me again. Anyway, I'm sorry, Neil. I really liked Courtney, and was hoping you'd see a future with her. If you really, really care about her—"

"I know. I know," he cut her off. "All right, I'll see her as soon as I fly back."

"When will that be?"

"I'm not sure. I have to finish some business before I can leave."

"Let me give you some sisterly advice," Maribeth said firmly. "You've held on to your shattered dreams with Wendy long enough. It's time to let go."

"I know, I know."

After he hung up, he ran an agitated hand through his hair, fighting a battle with himself. He had investors depending on him. He didn't see how he could cancel his important business conference.

Why was Courtney leaving? What the hell had happened?

COURTNEY SUMMONED HER COURAGE after dinner that evening, and told her aunt that she had decided to cut her vacation short.

"I know I planned to stay the summer, but I've changed my mind," Courtney said evenly. "I'll pack up our things tomorrow, and then get an early start back to Cheyenne the following morning."

"You can't. You can't just take off like that." Devanna clenched her fists and turned every shade of red.

"Why not?" Courtney asked in what she hoped was a reasonable tone. She had decided not to give her aunt much warning, hoping to avoid an extended quarrel between them.

"It's not time!"

"I think it is."

"No, no. It's too soon…too soon!"

"Let's not argue." Her aunt's dictatorial outburst only strengthened Courtney's resolve to leave. "I know you'll miss Jamie, and he'll miss you, but my mind is made up."

Clearly the only reason her aunt objected to her going was the baby. The tension had been increasing between them as every day passed. When Courtney exerted her rights to make motherly decisions that didn't meet Devanna's approval, her aunt's temper instantly flared. It was only a matter of time before they had a bitter quarrel. It was better all around to leave before that happened.

"What about that fellow of yours? Aren't you going to stick around till he gets back this weekend?"

"No, I'll leave Friday morning," she said firmly. Leaving before she saw Neil again was a coward's way out, but the break would be quicker and cleaner.

"Well, I suppose there's no sense wasting my breath." Devanna's eyes narrowed as if she were doing some heavy thinking.

"This just hasn't worked out," Courtney said as gently as she could.

"Oh, I don't know about that," Devanna retorted. "But anyway, there's still tomorrow, isn't there?"

Relieved that her aunt seemed to have reluctantly accepted her decision, Courtney began finalizing her departure. The next morning, she did all their washing and began to pack. As usual, Devanna ignored her and gave all her attention to the baby.

Toward late afternoon when Jamie went down for a nap, Courtney decided to enjoy one final sunbath on the roof.

"Good idea. You've been as pale as a bleached rag lately," her aunt commented with her usual bluntness.

As she put on her bathing suit, Courtney had a momentary flicker of regret. Even though the atmosphere inside the houseboat had been oppressive, outside the sun, the beautiful view of the lake, and the pleasant climate had offered her some enjoyable moments.

And then there was Neil.

She paused for a moment at the deck railing before climbing up to the roof. Looking across the water, she could see the usual panorama of boats and water-skiers on the lake. The memory of being with Neil in his boat, and their recent walk along the water's edge, created a swell of emotions. She'd never forget the way he made her feel when he smiled at her. The memory of his kisses sent a quiver of desire rippling through her. She could understand how devastating it would be to fall deeply in love with him, only to have him slip away.

Her eyes were misty as she turned away from the deck, and started to climb up the narrow ladder.

She made it nearly to the top.

Then it happened!

The ladder suddenly pulled away from its fastenings and she was flung backward.

She screamed as she hit the deck railing with such force that it broke, splintered and raked her arms and legs with deep cuts. One end of the falling ladder hit her head and propelled her over the side of the houseboat. Black water drew her down and down. Kicking and flailing her arms, she barely made it back to the surface.

"Help!" she cried out as she bobbed in the water, floundering like a wounded animal fighting to stay afloat. Blood from scratches and cuts turned the water red around her. Her head throbbed with blinding pain. Dizzy and filled with pain, she knew she couldn't last more than a few brief minutes. The only thing closer than the shore was the old rowboat tied up at the dock.

With blurry vision, she could see it bobbing in the water. She struck out, struggling to keep it in sight. Her few times in a swimming pool had scarcely been more than paddling in waist-high water. As she clumsily worked her arms and legs, her strokes weakened. She barely kept afloat. Her vision blurred and only raw determination kept her moving. It was only when her hands felt rough wood that she knew she had reached the rowboat.

With her last bit of strength, she pulled herself over the side of the boat. As she collapsed in the bottom, a rocking, floating sensation drew her away into unconsciousness.

Chapter Nine

Neil's flight was an hour late getting in to Manitou.
The sun was already setting behind the cluster of en-
veloping mountains when he picked up his recently
purchased car from the parking garage and drove
the fifteen miles to town. He had never before left a
business deal hanging unresolved the way he had that
afternoon. That important transaction demanded at
least two more full days of his time and energy.

"What's the matter with you?" his business associate had demanded when Neil's usual concentration
and dedication to business was obviously lacking.

"Personal problems," Neil had answered without
elaborating. "I'll get back to you in a day or two."

The flight was a short one, but to Neil it seemed
like an eternity.

*Courtney was leaving. Going out of his life as
suddenly as she'd come into it.*

He wrestled with emotions that made him a
stranger to himself. After he lost Wendy, he'd never
wanted to put his heart in jeopardy again. He'd been
careful in all his relationships to maintain a protec-

tive barrier against any deep, total commitment. His life had been shattered once, and he wasn't going to let it happen again, but he knew he'd be the worst kind of coward if he let Courtney disappear from his life without some kind of protest.

For the hundredth time he cursed the lack of a phone at the houseboat. He'd been tempted several times to offer to provide her with a cell phone, but feared her pride would take it as an insult. Just what argument he could use to keep her from leaving, he wasn't sure, but he had to try.

The late afternoon traffic was horrendous as he approached Manitou's city limits. A dozen stoplights diabolically turned red before he could get through. His impatience grew as he rehearsed in his mind his argument for her not to leave. He knew things were not harmonious with her aunt, but she could move out and stay someplace else. Money might be a factor, but he could arrange to pick up the difference—if she'd let him. When he remembered the firm set of her chin and the dogged independence she always displayed, he feared he wouldn't be able to change her mind.

When he reached Hidden Cove, Neil saw that Courtney's car was there, and was relieved she hadn't left yet. The gray van was gone.

Good, he thought. Devanna wouldn't be around to eavesdrop on their conversation. Something about the woman grated on his nerves.

The houseboat looked shut up as he crossed the dock and knocked on the door. Impatiently, he listened for some sound inside. A heavy stillness was broken only by the quiet rippling of the water against the boat.

Damn. She must have gone somewhere with her aunt. What should he do? Leave a note? No telling when they'd be back. He decided to check in at his office and come back a little later.

As he turned away from the door, a floating piece of deck railing caught his eye. Where'd that come from? Curious, he walked around the corner of the houseboat.

"What the hell?"

The sight that met his eyes stunned him.

The railing had a gaping hole and the ladder was snagged on one of the broken boards. As he came closer, a torn scrap of a pink bathing suit spattered with blood curdled his insides.

No! His heart stopped as his terrified gaze searched the water.

"Courtney! Courtney!" He shouted her name as he began circling the houseboat. No sign of her in the water. Maybe she was inside. Hurt.

He tried the door. It was unlocked and he called her name as he hurried inside. No sign of her or the baby. The splatters of blood on the wood outside were evidence that she'd been hurt. Maybe her aunt had taken her to the hospital?

As he hurried out on the deck again, he almost missed a faint whimpering that was scarcely more than a whisper.

He froze and listened. Had his ears been playing a trick on him? Was it coming from the rowboat tied against the dock a short distance away? He ran over to it.

"Courtney! My God!"

Bruised, bloody and nearly drowned, she lay in a heap on the bottom of the boat. She was barely conscious, and whimpering as he gathered her into his arms.

NEIL FOLLOWED THE AMBULANCE to the hospital and waited anxiously in the emergency room. The smells and sounds of the hospital were painfully familiar because he'd spent many hours at Wendy's bedside when she was dying. Despite all his vows not to let himself love anyone deeply again, it had happened. Courtney had moved into that empty place in his heart. He'd begun to let the barriers down, and hopes for a future with someone he could dearly love seemed a reality. When the doctor finally appeared, Neil prepared himself to hear the worst.

"She's lost a lot of blood, but fortunately her wounds are not deep," the young doctor assured him. "No broken bones, only a couple of bruised ribs. The most serious injury is a slight concussion. We'll have to watch her closely until the swelling goes down."

"But she's going to be all right?" Relief rippled through him.

"If she takes care of herself. No doubt, she's going to be uncomfortable for a while."

"Can I see her?"

"A few minutes, but no more. She's conscious now, but we'll be keeping her sedated for the first twenty-four hours."

Neil hesitated at the hospital room door for a minute as he absorbed the shock of seeing Courtney hooked up to IVs, and lying listless with bandages all over.

A nurse hovered close by as Neil approached the bed and bent over her. As he took her hand, she gingerly turned her bandaged head to look at him.

"How you doing, sweetheart?"

She gave him a weak smile.

During the torturous wait in the emergency room, he'd asked himself over and over how such a thing could have happened. He knew Courtney had been climbing up and down that ladder almost every day to sunbathe. Somehow the screws holding it must have worked loose and flung her backward.

A chill crept up his spine as he realized how easily she could have drowned. It was a miracle she had made it to the safety of the boat. She'd never have had the strength to climb up on the dock.

"You're going to be fine," he assured her, even as her pale face and glazed eyes wrenched his heart. "The doctor just wants you to rest."

"Jamie?" she whispered in a cracked voice.

"I'll make sure he's all right."

"Maribeth?"

"Sure, my sister will look after him if that's what you want."

She moistened her lips. "Devanna…won't… like…it."

"Don't worry, I'll handle her."

The nurse nodded at him.

He kissed Courtney lightly on the forehead. "Don't worry, darling. I'll make sure everything is all right. You just sleep and get well."

His promise seemed to satisfy her. A kind of peace settled on her drawn face. The nurse stepped forward to give her a sedative.

Neil waited until Courtney's eyes closed and long eyelashes fringed her pale cheeks before he turned and left the room. As he drove back to the houseboat, he began to make plans.

He'd pick up Jamie and take him to Maribeth so she could care for him while Courtney was in the hospital. No doubt Devanna would vigorously object. Even though Courtney had told Neil how devoted Devanna was to the baby, he knew her aunt's unpredictable behavior had been a worry to her. Neil was determined to put Courtney's mind at ease about Jamie's care, and steeled himself for an unpleasant scene with her aunt.

Night had settled on the mountain valley, and five hours had passed since he'd rushed Courtney to the hospital. When he arrived at the houseboat, he was surprised when Courtney's car was still the only one in the parking area. Either Devanna hadn't returned, or she'd come and gone.

He couldn't see any sign of a light as he descended the stairs and crossed the dock. The houseboat looked dark and deserted. He knocked on the door and called out Devanna's name, but there was no response.

The door was still unlocked. He turned on a light, and this time the condition of the houseboat hit him. When he'd raced through it earlier, he'd been so intent on finding Courtney that he'd been oblivious to everything else. Now he was aware that signs of

hasty packing were everywhere. He knew that Courtney had been packing up to leave, but why would the
whole houseboat be in such shambles? Cupboard
doors in the galley were ajar. The food shelves
looked strangely empty.

His chest began to tighten as he looked in Devanna's compartment and saw the nearly empty clothes
closet. When he looked around for the baby's
belongings and didn't see any, the truth hit him with
the force of a blow to the stomach.

Devanna had moved out! With the baby!

He dialed McGrady's office on his cell phone,
and fortunately the detective was still there.

Neil poured out his mounting anxiety. "Courtney
had an accident this afternoon. She's in the hospital,
and wanted me to check on the baby. I found the
place deserted. Nobody here." Neil's voice rose to
angry pitch. "Her aunt's moved out. I don't know
where in the hell she's gone, but she's got the baby
with her."

"Hey, slow down. I'll be there in a few minutes."

When McGrady arrived, he wandered through the
houseboat with his usual slow, measured pace as
Neil pointed out the moving mess. "It's damn clear!
She's taken food, her clothes, and everything of
Jamie's."

"You may be jumping to conclusions, Neil," McGrady cautioned. "Maybe the two women agreed to
move out of the houseboat while you were out of
town."

"My sister told me Courtney was planning on
leaving Manitou in a few days."

"Isn't it possible she'd been helping her aunt move to another place, and wasn't able to think clearly enough in the hospital to tell you?"

Neil began to relax a little. Maybe he was jumping to conclusions too damn fast, but something didn't add up. "Where was Devanna when Courtney got hurt this afternoon?"

"Tell me more about this accident of hers," Mc-Grady said. "When did it happen?"

"I don't know for sure," Neil admitted. "Sometime before late afternoon when I got here. Her doctor could probably give you a better estimate."

After turning on the deck lights, he showed Mc-Grady the fallen ladder and broken railing. "Courtney liked to climb up on the roof and sunbathe. When the ladder pulled away, she was flung overboard. Thank God she managed to stay afloat and reach the rowboat, even with her injuries."

She could have just as easily drowned.

"The aunt must have been gone, or the ladder falling and breaking the deck railing would have alerted her," McGrady speculated.

"You would think so," Neil agreed but without conviction. He'd witnessed Devanna's self-absorbed and self-centered personality.

McGrady stared up at the place where the ladder screws had come out of the wall. "Maybe I'll have someone take a closer look tomorrow."

"Why? You don't think—?"

"I try not to think anything until I have some concrete evidence in my hands. Saves a lot of time going down the wrong road." There was a warning in his tone that indicated Neil ought to do likewise. "I would like to have a chat with the aunt, though. I'll put out an APB on her van. When we locate her, we'll probably be able to clear up a lot of this in short order."

"We'd better! They're going to keep Courtney sedated for a while. I need to have some reassurances for her about the baby when she comes out of it."

"You and that lady friend of yours have had more than your share of trauma and drama, recently." He gave Neil a reassuring pat on the shoulder. "Hang in there. I'll call you as soon as I have something. Manitou isn't that big. We should be able to locate the aunt within twenty-four hours."

The relief that McGrady promised was not forthcoming in the next twenty-four hours—nor the day after that. The local APB brought no results, and McGrady called Neil with even more devastating information.

"I'm afraid I have some disturbing news about Courtney's accident. Our experts have verified that the screws holding the ladder had been loosened so that her weight would pull it away from the wall. Her fall was no accident, Neil. It was deliberate."

COURTNEY FLOATED to the surface of consciousness repeatedly only to sink again into sedated nothingness. As the gray fog began to lift, she became aware of hushed sounds, vague movements around her and the sure touch of hands upon her body. As her heavy eyelids fluttered upward, she struggled to bring images of light and dark into focus.

"She's coming out of it."

"Notify the doctor."

"Take it easy, honey." A comforting hand patted her arm. "You're in good hands. Don't you worry about anything," the motherly voice advised. "We'll take good care of you."

Courtney didn't have the strength to voice the questions that plagued her. Closing her heavy eyelids, she kept floating away into a blessed state of renewing sleep.

The next time she awoke, her vision was clearer, and she turned her head toward a figure sitting by her bed. Neil's face came into focus, and a quiver of unbelievable relief rippled through her.

"Hi." Bending over her, he smoothed back lank hair from her forehead. "How are you feeling?"

"Better now." Her lips were stiff. She tried to draw on memories that evaded her. She looked at Neil with questioning eyes. "I'm in the hospital?"

"Yes, you had an—accident."

"Accident?" she echoed.

As evenly as he could, he said, "The ladder on the houseboat gave way. You broke the deck railing and fell into the water."

Pieces of her memory suddenly whirled like a maelstrom. His words ignited the fear, the struggle, the pain as she'd fought to stay afloat.

Her eyes deepened in remembered fright, and he leaned forward and kissed her wan cheek. "You're safe now, darling. You just need to rest."

"How long have I been here?"

"Three days."

Her eyes rounded. "Jamie? He's with Maribeth?"

Neil had been dreading that question. The doctor had warned him that even a simple concussion could be exacerbated by continued emotional stress, and any sudden trauma might affect her recovery. Neil had decided it would be better to lie to her until she had left the hospital, but would she ever forgive him for not being completely honest with her?

"Yes," he answered, evading the horrid truth that Devanna had moved out, taking the baby with her. The callous deceit of the woman sickened and frightened Neil. How could he possibly tell Courtney that Jamie was in the hands of such a deranged person?

"The doctor expects you to be released in the next day or two, so try not to worry." *I'm doing enough of that for both of us.*

"You'll make sure Jamie's all right?"

"Sweetheart, I'll do anything I can to make sure you and Jamie are safe." He hoped she wouldn't notice that he sidestepped a direct answer. "As soon as you're better, we have to talk about us."

"Us?"

"Yes, us. Like you and me and Jamie."

She couldn't help but smile at the fantasy even if it proved to be short-lived. Neil was obviously shaken by what had happened, and emotions that ran high during a crisis usually returned to normal when it was over. There would be time enough to face reality when she was well enough to take charge of the baby, and leave Manitou as she'd planned.

"How's my aunt taking all of this?"

"Just as you might expect," he answered, praying

they'd find the blasted woman and have the baby back before Courtney knew he was missing.

After leaving the hospital, Neil went directly to the police station. When he walked into McGrady's office, he knew the situation hadn't changed.

"Every lead we've had on a gray van has been a dead end," the detective told him. "Our earlier assumption that Devanna moved out of the houseboat to a different location in town hasn't borne fruit. I've had an officer posted in case she came back to the houseboat, but we're pretty certain she left for good. We've extended our APB nationwide."

Neil's heart sank. In three days the woman could be halfway across the country, or across the Canadian border, only a short day's drive from Manitou.

"How's Courtney doing?"

"She's out of the induced coma now."

"Good. Maybe she'll be able to give us some information that will help."

Neil said quickly, "I didn't tell her about the baby being gone. I just couldn't. If you hit her with that now, no telling how she'll react."

"She'll have to know sometime," McGrady said gently.

"I was hoping we'd find Devanna before Courtney had to face the truth."

"I'm sorry but it doesn't look as if that's going to happen. If we don't hit pay dirt in the first thirty-six hours, we usually have to settle for a slow, piece-by-piece resolution of a case. Kidnapping is the worst torture for everyone."

"At least we know who has the baby," Neil said.

"It's not some stranger but his own flesh and blood. You know, Devanna didn't strike me as smart enough to pull off something like this."

"We're going over the houseboat with everything forensics can offer."

Even as he spoke, his secretary came in with a computer printout. "It's the fingerprint confirmation you've been waiting for."

She glanced at Neil as she handed it to McGrady and then left the office. McGrady leaned forward in his chair, holding the report in his large hands. As he read, his jaw hardened and his eyes narrowed. When he had finished, he laid the papers down and leaned toward Neil.

"The fingerprint check came up with some surprising and disturbing evidence."

"What do you mean?"

"We were able to obtain Devanna Davenport's fingerprints from a legal report she made a few years back. We used it to compare with the ones we found in the houseboat."

"And?" Neil prodded, trying to hurry up the man's slow, methodical way of speaking.

"Funny thing," he mused. "They don't match any we found in the houseboat."

"What? How is that possible?"

"Courtney's aunt Devanna was never in that houseboat. Or if she was, it wasn't for very long. The fingerprints belong to a Billie Mae Kessel, a wanted fugitive who has already served time for robbery early in her lawless career. Her accomplice was killed during a thwarted robbery attempt several months ago. She successfully evaded the police and, obviously, has been in hiding since then."

For a choked minute, Neil just stared at the detective. When he found his voice, he stammered, " You mean—you mean this woman, Kessel, has been pretending to be Courtney's aunt?"

"Looks that way."

"And the real Devanna Davenport?"

McGrady just shook his head. The obvious, ugly answer was like a foul miasma filling the room, making Neil sick to his stomach.

Chapter Ten

McGrady's brow furrowed as he looked across his desk at Neil. "We've got to put a different frame around everything that's happened."

Neil's mind was in a tailspin. He wanted to protest that surely there'd been a mistake. This couldn't be true.

"Did the real Devanna rent the houseboat from your company or did Billie Mae?" McGrady asked.

Neil forced himself to focus on the question. "Everything was handled by mail. The address on the correspondence was a suburb of Seattle. I know because I looked into the rental when I decided to show up at the houseboat, and introduce myself to Courtney."

"So no one in your office ever saw Devanna Davenport? I'll call Seattle and have them do a background check on her." McGrady looked thoughtful. "I wonder when the switch took place? After the aunt got here? Or before? Either way, Billie Mae could have arranged to get her out of the picture before Courtney arrived."

Neil's stomach took a sickening plunge. "Killed her?"

"Nothing else makes much sense, does it?" Mc-Grady agreed sadly. "She couldn't afford to have anyone around who knew she wasn't the real De-vanna Davenport."

Neil stared at the detective for a long moment as his mind whirled like a slot machine about to hit a jackpot. Then he leaned forward in his chair. "Har-old Jensen. He knew the real Devanna."

"I'll be damned," McGrady swore. "That's it!"

"It was a lie that he never came back to the houseboat."

"Right. No wonder we never got to first base in his murder investigation. We were looking in the wrong places for a motive. Billie Mae had to elimi-nate him because he knew she was an impostor."

Now it all made sense to Neil.

"Jensen shows up at the houseboat, expecting to see his old friend, and instead he gets shot and dumped in the lake."

McGrady nodded in agreement. "If that storm hadn't washed his body up, we might never have known what happened to him."

"Courtney's life was at risk from the first moment she arrived, wasn't it?" A cold shiver rippled through him.

"Looks that way, doesn't it?"

"At anytime, Courtney could have stumbled on the truth that this woman was not her aunt. She was innocently living with a murderer, and didn't know it."

McGrady was silent as he rubbed his chin. Then his eyes lit up. "That's it!"

"What?"

"The connection I've been looking for! This information puts a different light on that narrow escape you and Courtney had on the mountain."

"You mean it wasn't Delaney and Woodword?" Neil had settled on them as the guilty ones.

"We never came up with any proof against them," McGrady admitted. "They landed in jail because of other illegal activities. I'm betting when we find Billie Mae Kessel, we'll have the gun that shot out your tires—and the one that killed Jensen."

Neil rested his head in his hands and groaned. "How am I going to tell Courtney all of this?"

"She's a strong woman," McGrady reminded him. "Look at the way she handled that near-death experience on the mountain."

"But this is different," Neil protested. "Her baby is in the hands of a woman who's killed before, and who tried to kill her."

"I'm betting Courtney has an inner strength that will see her through."

"I'll have to tell her before she leaves the hospital in a day or two. She thinks Jamie is safely with my sister." Neil's mouth went dry. "She'll be totally devastated."

"Well, we may get lucky and find the baby before she knows the truth," McGrady said hopefully, but something in his tone warned Neil it wasn't very likely.

COURTNEY WAS SITTING UP in bed when Neil came to the hospital the next day. Her spirits instantly rose when she saw him. The doctor had just told her that she was going to be released, and she was feeling surprisingly fit.

"You're spoiling me," she teased when he handed her a beautiful bouquet of flowers, his third in as many days.

"You're worth spoiling," he assured her as he sat down on the edge of the bed. Leaning over, he kissed her gently on the lips and caressed her cheek lightly with his fingertips. "If there's anything you need, want, just let me know."

Looking up at him, she suddenly became aware of how terrible he looked. Stress lines tightened the corners of his mouth. Dark shadows deepened the distressed look in his eyes. He looked like a man who hadn't slept in days.

"Don't look so worried. I'm fine," she assured him. "The doctor says I'll be released tomorrow."

"Tomorrow?" he echoed.

"What's the matter? Don't you think that's good news," she chided when she saw a deepening of concern in his expression. "I can hardly wait to get back to spoiling my baby."

Taking a deep breath and summoning his courage, he told her the truth as quickly and kindly as he could about the woman she thought was Devanna Davenport.

"We don't know what happened to your real aunt. We only know that this woman, Billie Mae Kessel, took her place at some point before you got here."

She stared at him in total shock. "No."

"I'm afraid it's true. All of it."

"It can't be." Even as she heard herself protesting, some part of her knew he spoke the horrible truth. All the clues to the deception had been there from the beginning, and she'd been blind to them.

"And there's more," Neil warned. There was no way to soften the blow. He had to just come out and say it. "She disappeared the day you fell, and she took Jamie with her."

She stared at him blankly. "No, Jamie's with Maribeth," she corrected him.

Neil slowly shook his head.

"Yes he is! You said so."

"I know, but you have to understand," he pleaded. "You weren't in any condition to handle the truth. When I went back to the houseboat to get him, the place was empty."

"We have to find him!" She threw back the covers and started to get out of bed.

"McGrady has the whole police force on alert." Neil put firm hands on her shoulders and lowered her back onto the pillows. "They'll find Jamie and bring him back."

"How can you be sure?" She covered her face with her hands and her shoulders shook with sobs.

"The woman won't hurt Jamie. She loves him. She'll take care of him. You saw how good she was with him. She'll keep him safe."

Unless the woman's own safety is threatened. Then who knew what she'd do? Neil pushed away the thought.

Tears spilled down her cheeks. What a blind fool

she'd been. All that shopping had been in preparation for the kidnapping. Devanna had been getting ready to steal Jamie from right under Courtney's nose.

"McGrady is optimistic. It won't be long before they track her down," Neil assured her as he wiped away her tears. "They've put out an all-points bulletin. We'll find her and get Jamie back, safe and sound. In the meantime, I'm taking you home with me."

Courtney had neither the energy nor inclination to argue. What did it matter? She'd just be marking time until she got her baby back. There would be time soon enough to try and put her life back together again.

MARIBETH WAS AT NEIL'S HOUSE when they arrived the next morning. As she came hurrying out to the car, Neil saw tears in his sister's eyes, and sent her a warning look. Courtney had been remarkably brave dealing with the devastating situation. McGrady had been right about her, Courtney possessed a lot of inner strength.

"I'm so sorry," Maribeth said, blinking rapidly as they walked toward his front door.

"Thank you for the clothes," Courtney said, indicating the new jeans, matching denim blouse, and sandals Maribeth had sent to the hospital with Neil, along with some personal toiletries, in a small overnight bag.

Since the houseboat had been declared a crime scene, Courtney had been advised that she couldn't remove any of her possessions until the authorities had finished with it.

"It was a pleasure shopping for you," Maribeth assured her. "I put a few other things in the guest closet and bathroom. If there's anything I missed, just let me know."

Neil saw that Courtney was struggling to accept this kind of charity. Undoubtedly, under other circumstances she would have exerted her independence and refused help. He respected that wonderful pride of hers, but was determined to take care of her whether she liked it or not.

"As I said, I made up the guest room for you," Maribeth said, and sent Neil a defiant look.

Neil got her message, but he'd never intended for Courtney to share his room or his bed. She needed her own space and he knew it. It was enough just to have her safely under the same roof.

"Do you want to rest now? Have lunch a little later?" he asked.

Courtney nodded. "If that's okay?"

"Anything you want is okay."

"You just tell us," Maribeth insisted.

Neil put his arm around Courtney's waist, and she wondered if he were remembering that last time they were on these stairs. Was it a lifetime ago that her body was flushed with desire, the moment shattered by the ring of a doorbell? None of what had happened that day seemed real now. She was grateful for a protective detachment as they passed his room and walked down the hall to the guest suite.

"I'll catch up on some computer work while

Maribeth gets you settled. If there's anything you need—"

"I'll take care of it, brother, dear." Maribeth gave him a playful shove. "Fix yourself a drink, and relax." She shook her head after he left and turned to Courtney "These last few days have been pure hell for him. He's been torn up with worry. I guess you know by now, he's not taking your relationship lightly."

Courtney sighed. "I don't think we have what you call a 'relationship.'"

"Then why is he so devastated by what has happened? Since your accident, he's been behaving the same way he did when he was about to lose Wendy. His life collapsed then, and he shut down emotionally. I hate to see that happening again."

"I don't know what I would do without his support," Courtney admitted.

Maribeth sat down beside her on the bed, and asked bluntly, "How deep are your feelings for my brother?"

"I don't know," Courtney answered honestly. At the moment, she was using all of her emotional reserves to cope with the kidnapping of her child.

Something in Courtney's voice must have touched Maribeth because she apologized quickly. "I have no right to push you like this. That's one of my weaknesses. Always trying to fix things that are none of my business. I'm sorry."

"No, I understand. Neil's lucky to have a sister like you," Courtney replied honestly. The present crisis had made her realize how barren her life was of people who really cared about her. If it wasn't for Neil and his family, she'd be totally alone.

"He might argue about how lucky he is," Maribeth answered with a faint smile. "Now, that's enough talk."

She opened the closet and showed Courtney several garments hanging there: a soft robe and matching pajamas, a summer print skirt, two blouses and a belted cotton sweater. "There are a few other things in the drawers that will tide you over until you feel like shopping."

Courtney felt a catch in her throat as she thanked her.

"No big deal," Maribeth said, with a dismissing wave of her hand. "Why don't you stretch out and rest while I go downstairs and see what kind of lunch I can scare up in the bachelor's kitchen?"

Neil met Maribeth at the bottom of the stairs. "What do you think? Is she going to be all right?"

"I don't know what you mean by all right," Maribeth answered. "If someone ran off with one of my kids, I don't think I'd ever be 'all right.' One thing's for sure, I'd move heaven and hell to get them back, and I think Courtney's the same way. She's a fighter."

"Yes, she is," Neil agreed. He'd been amazed at her resilience in the face of such a heartbreak.

"I sure wouldn't want to be in that woman's shoes when Courtney catches up with her. McGrady's pretty confident about tracking her down, isn't he?"

"When he thought he was dealing with Courtney's aunt, he was, but Billie Mae is an experienced criminal. She knows how to evade the law. It may take time—a lot of time."

"What will Courtney do in the meantime? Is she going to stay here?"

"I hope so," he replied, but he wasn't at all sure Courtney would stay a minute longer than necessary. She'd been ready to leave Manitou while he was out of town, and if that was an indication of the depth of her feelings for him, she wouldn't be comfortable living in the same house. "We'll just have to wait and see."

Courtney came down about an hour later. Even though she was emotionally tired, she hadn't been able to sleep, and she hated being alone.

"Lunch is ready," Maribeth said brightly when she entered the kitchen. "Neil set the table out on the terrace."

Courtney knew Neil and Maribeth were doing their best to handle an almost intolerable situation. They would never know how much their tender care strengthened her. They seemed to know when to remain silent and when to speak words of comfort.

The three of them were just finishing lunch when they heard a car drive up in the driveway. Neil shot Maribeth a questioning look. Who could that be? Were some well-meaning family members going to intrude on Courtney's privacy?

"I'll see who that is." Neil rose quickly to his feet and made his way through the house to the front door, ready to turn away any good-intentioned visitors. He peeked through the pane of glass and saw McGrady's unmarked van in the driveway.

He quickly opened the door, his heart racing. Had the detective come in person to give them good news? Neil tried to read McGrady's expression as he mounted the front steps. No hint of a smile on the detective's weathered face, and his slow, ambling walk was the same. Neil's hopes fell.

McGrady's nod of greeting was apologetic. "Glad to find you home. The hospital said Courtney is staying with you. I need to have her look at something."

"She's on the terrace with my sister."

"Where's your VCR?"

Neil motioned toward the den. "Why don't you go on in. Have a seat. I'll go get her."

When he told Courtney that McGrady was there, she had the same reaction as he had. Her face flushed and her eyes lost their dead look.

"He wants you to look at something."

"What?" Her face paled.

"A video, I think," he answered quickly.

"What kind of video?" his sister asked in her usual forthright manner.

"I don't know, but it must be important." Neil took Courtney's hand in his and gave it a reassuring squeeze. "Let's go find out."

McGrady was standing in front of Neil's entertainment center when they came in. As Courtney walked over to him, he responded to her hopeful, pleading look with a shake of his head. He didn't have to say anything. Courtney knew her baby was still missing.

"Please sit down. There's been a new development that we need to track. When the investigators were going through the houseboat they found some blue paper bands in the suspect's sleeping cabin. Billie Mae Kessel has a record of bank robberies, and these blue bands are the kind Capital Bank uses to bundle their paper currency."

"She robbed the bank?" Neil asked in utter surprise.

"It looks that way. I've brought the bank's video to show you, Courtney. Maybe there's some betraying mannerism or detail that you will recognize." He softened his tone. "Do you feel up to it?"

"I'll do anything I can to help."

She tried to settle her queasy stomach as they loaded the VCR and ran the tape. She didn't know what she expected to see, but the whiskered man in the cowboy hat brought no recognition at all.

Courtney was about to shake her head when her gaze focused on the gloved hand holding the gun. Some of the stitching on the back was different from the rest, and in a clear flashback, Courtney remembered her "aunt" mending a leather glove like that. Because this domestic act had been so contrary to her usual behavior it had made an impression on Courtney.

"The glove."

"What about it?" McGrady quickly put the tape on a still frame.

"It had a rip in it, and she used a black thread to mend the tear, instead of brown."

"Good girl," McGrady said, pleased. "We'll get an enlargement of the glove to verify it."

It was then that Neil remembered there had been

something familiar about the robber's physical stature when he'd watched the news the night of the robbery. If he'd honored his intuition, he might have connected it with the same feeling "Devanna" gave him.

"Will this help find this woman?" Maribeth asked McGrady.

"Bank robbery is a federal offense, and that means more law enforcement agencies will be involved in the case," McGrady explained. "But there's a downside to this discovery," he warned.

Courtney stiffened. How could the situation be made any worse than before? "What do you mean?"

"Billie isn't hurting for money. Her take in that robbery was considerable. She's well padded. No telling how long she can hole up somewhere."

"But there's a good chance she'll be spending a lot of that money to cover her tracks," Neil argued. "And someone will notice."

"If they do, you can bet we'll be on it," he promised. He stood up and walked over to where Courtney was sitting on the couch. "I have six little ones of my own. You can be damn sure I'll be on this the same way I would be if it were one of my own." He patted her hand. "I'll be going now. Thank you for your help."

Neil walked with him to the door. "What have you found out about Courtney's real aunt?"

"Not much," McGrady admitted. "Devanna Davenport was a real recluse. From everything we've learned, she didn't go out much, and, apparently, didn't have any close friends in Seattle. How and when Billie hooked up with her we aren't quite sure.

"A service station near her home where she bought gas gave us our only lead. The attendant said he remembered filling the gray van with gas about a month ago because it was there waiting for him when he opened up the station. There were two women in the van. One he identified as Billie, the other was probably the real Devanna."

"Then they left Seattle together?"

"It would seem so," the detective agreed. "What happened between that time, and the evening Courtney showed up at the houseboat, we haven't a clue." He sighed. "And I'm afraid we won't—until we find a body. We're pretty confident she's the one who shot Jensen and dumped his body in the lake. It might be a pattern."

"I won't tell Courtney. She never really knew her aunt so her disappearance is easier to bear. It's her son's kidnapping that's tearing her apart."

"We'll follow up on any lead we get," McGrady promised as he took his leave.

When Neil returned to the den, it was empty. He found Maribeth gathering up her things in the kitchen, preparing to leave. She told him that Courtney had gone upstairs to her room.

"I don't know how she can handle all of this. We've got to help all we can. You call me anytime, day or night." Maribeth frowned as she looked at him. "You don't look all that great yourself."

He gave her an affectionate squeeze. "Thanks, sis. You really know how to build a man's ego."

"You've never had any trouble in that department," she chided, smiling. "Don't try to handle this all by yourself. Everyone wants to do what they can to help. You let us know."

He promised he would.

After he'd helped her into her car and watched her drive away, he stood on the porch and surveyed the panoramic view that stretched from the lake to the encircling mountains. He could see the silver ribbons of highways stretching east to Montana, west to the Pacific Coast and north to the Canadian border.

As he stood in the warm sunshine, he fought a bone-deep, consuming chill. It had been almost four days since the deranged woman had disappeared.

By now she could be anywhere.

Chapter Eleven

Courtney didn't come back downstairs, so Neil took her up a tray at dinnertime, which she only pretended to eat. Every time he stopped at the bedroom door and looked in on her, she had her eyes closed, but he suspected from her rigid form that she was feigning sleep.

He stayed downstairs until almost midnight, working at his computer, trying to catch up on office work. He had just gone upstairs and was getting ready for bed when he heard Courtney cry out.

Barefoot and wearing only his trousers, he hurried into her room. Courtney was curled up in a ball, her face moist with tears, and her fists pressed against her mouth, trying to stifle her sobbing. Her shivering body was cold to the touch and she was breathing rapidly. He wondered if she was reliving those moments in the chilled water, fighting for her life.

"It's all right, darling. You're safe." He quickly slipped under the covers beside her and pulled her trembling body close to his.

Courtney heard his voice and fought her way out

of the nightmare that had enveloped her. His touch was reassuring, but as reality rushed back, her anguish only increased. How much longer could she stand not knowing about her baby? Was Jamie really all right? Would "Devanna" continue to love and care for him?

"It's my fault," she sobbed. "I should have guarded my baby better."

"Stop that," he ordered gently as he cradled her head against his chest. "None of this is your fault."

"But—I was so blind."

"No, just trusting," he softly corrected her. "You accepted everything at face value, and why not? You thought she was your aunt."

Courtney shivered. "I wanted her to like me. I tried to please her, and all the time she was planning on taking my baby away from me."

She remembered how pleased she'd been when her "aunt" had started being nice to her, but it all made sense now. The woman had just been setting the stage to get rid of her. Courtney's lips trembled. "She must have tried to poison me."

Neil silently swore at his own blindness. How stupid he'd been to believe the restaurant had been responsible for the bad clam chowder. He knew now when the poisoned soup didn't work, "Devanna" had arranged the ladder accident.

"All this time she wanted me dead, and I didn't know it." She clung to him with the fierceness of someone who knew it was a miracle she was still alive.

"You were too strong for her." Neil breathed a

prayer of thankfulness as her warm body rested against his. How easily he could have lost her. If any of the murderous impostor's plans had succeeded, Courtney could have tragically been another one of her victims.

His hand gently lifted moist hair from her cheeks, and he brushed her forehead with his lips. He doubted that she'd had more than a few hours rest since she came out of her sedated coma.

"Try to get some sleep."

"Stay with me?"

"As long as you like."

She startled him when she turned over so that his body cupped hers like spoons as they lay together. The position was an intimate one, and he wondered if his fortitude was going to be strong enough to deflect the feelings it aroused.

She seemed oblivious to the test she was imposing upon him. Almost like a child nestled in his arms, her breathing slowly deepened as it eased into the even rhythm of sleep. He wondered at the contentment he felt just holding her.

Once she stirred and cried out, and he soothed her back to sleep. He didn't know how long he lay awake but when he awoke the light of early morning was framed in the drawn curtains. For a moment he'd forgotten where he'd spent the night. As he turned his head, he was startled to find himself alone in bed.

The bathroom door was open, and no sign of Courtney. Going back to his room, he put on fresh jeans and a short-sleeve summer shirt. Then he hurried down the stairs. Even before he reached the bottom step, he smelled coffee.

When he entered the kitchen, Courtney was sitting at the round table near the windows, a coffee mug in one hand and a piece of toast in the other.

She looked embarrassed as if she didn't know quite how to greet him. "Hey."

"Good morning. You're an early bird," he chided, smiling.

She looked better than she had the day before, physically stronger and more rested. A welcoming sense of relief sluiced through him.

"I woke up hungry," she confessed.

"I'm not surprised. You didn't eat much last night. I see you've already found the coffeemaker. What can I fix you for breakfast?" He winked at her. "I make a mean omelet. Specialty of the house."

As she watched his strongly masculine figure move easily about the kitchen, his debonair attitude reminded her that he was used to having feminine company at breakfast. She felt a pang of jealousy that had no place in the present situation. His comforting last night had been without any romantic overtones. When she'd awakened in his arms, there'd been a momentary longing within her, but she'd slipped out of bed before such thoughts could take hold.

As they ate breakfast, Courtney did her best to keep the conversation general. Like someone stepping around dangerous quicksand, she closed her mind to the constant churning anxiety within her. She asked about his company, and assured him that he didn't need to stay away from the office on her account.

"In fact, I have some things I want to do," she told him. "I'd appreciate it if you'd drop me off at the houseboat."

He was obviously startled. "Do you think that's a good idea?"

"I want to pick up my car, for one thing. And McGrady said forensics had finished, so I can go back to the houseboat."

Neil quickly grabbed her hand. "But I want you to stay here. With me. There's no need for you to go back to the houseboat. My house is your house, Courtney, until Jamie is safely back in your arms."

The relief on her face was instantaneous. "Thank you. I was hoping you would say that. But I do need to go collect my things."

"I'm sure Maribeth would be willing to do that for you."

"Probably, but I'd rather do it myself." She didn't tell him her real reason. There was a chance she might find some clue in the houseboat to Billie Kessel's whereabouts that the police had overlooked.

Neil saw the determined lift of her chin and knew it wouldn't do him any good to argue. In a way, he was relieved to see her focused and displaying more energy. Only a few ugly scratches and bruises on her arms were reminders of her close call. It amazed him how quickly she had recovered from her ordeal.

"All right. We'll stop at the office, and pick up a key to the houseboat. I'm sure the police left it locked up tight. After you collect your things, I'll follow you in your car back here."

His tone didn't invite any argument, and she wasn't about to give him one. She knew what a blessing it was that he'd taken her in. She couldn't even imagine how she would function without his strong support.

NEIL CLOSED HIS MIND against the vision of the crumpled mass of metal at the bottom of a rocky ravine and gave Courtney a concerned look as he pulled into the parking area above the houseboat. "Are you all right?"

She didn't answer for a moment, fighting a rising nausea that churned her stomach. Maybe this wasn't a good idea after all. She wasn't sure she had the courage to walk down those steps into that loathsome houseboat once more. Everything would remind her of Jamie and the painful emptiness she felt.

Neil sensed her hesitation and put his arm around her shoulder. "You can change your mind, you know."

"No, I can't," she answered, swallowing hard.

"Why not?"

"Because…because maybe I'll find something that will tell me where my baby is."

Neil saw the firm jut of her chin, and knew why she was willing to put herself through all kinds of mental and emotional torture. She'd convinced herself she would find something the police had missed. He feared she'd set herself up for another wrenching disappointment, but he knew better than to try to dissuade her.

Courtney was grateful for his guiding hand as they descended the narrow steps. When they stepped on the dock, her eyes went to the rowboat that was still tethered at the side of the houseboat. Ugly blotches of blood stained the bottom, and she shivered, remembering.

Neil quickly unlocked the door, and as he flung it open, an unpleasant, dank miasma floated out from the dark interior. He shot a quick look at Courtney. As he watched her face take on a sickly pallor, he cursed himself for having given in to her stubbornness.

"Are you all right? Are you sure you want to do this?"

She straightened her shoulders. "Yes."

The place was in shambles. Furniture had been turned upside down, bookcases and cupboards emptied, and even the walls bore signs of careful scrutiny.

"It doesn't look to me like the police missed anything," Neil said, hoping to offer some reassurance and get her out of there as soon as possible.

A cold rage rose in Courtney as she stood in the middle of the sitting room and remembered the treachery that had been heaped upon her. She saw the deceitful "Devanna" everywhere she looked. How could she have innocently entrusted her baby to such a monster?

"How could I have been so blind?"

"Easy. Easy," Neil cautioned, touching her arm. "Get the things you want, and let's get out of here."

Without answering, she walked past him to the

doorway of her sleeping compartment. The bunk beds had been stripped, the small closet emptied, and her clothes piled in a heap on the floor. Even her purse had been opened, and the contents spilled on the bed.

The empty room tore at the heart. Everything belonging to the baby was missing except for a couple of toys and some soiled blankets. She remembered how "Devanna" had shown off all the new things she'd bought for Jamie.

Courtney clung to the reassurance that everything that Jamie needed had been taken with him. She had to believe the woman was as conscientious about his care as she'd been when posing as Devanna, or she'd go crazy just thinking about it.

"Let me help you pack," Neil volunteered as he set her two empty suitcases on the bed.

She nodded. "Everything in here is mine, and the things on the bottom shelf of the bathroom sink."

Turning away, she went into the sleeping cabin that had been occupied by the impostor. There were still clothes and personal possessions in piles on the bed and in the closet. As she went through them, she realized they didn't match anything she'd seen Billie wear or use. They were the style her real aunt must have worn. Whatever had belonged to Billie Kessel was gone.

Neil leaned against the door frame, watching her. "What are you looking for?"

"I'm not sure." Her hope of uncovering any clue as to her baby's whereabouts had been the fancy of a desperate mother. She knew it, and so did Neil. She could almost hear the woman's laughter mocking her as she went back into the sitting area.

When she slipped a baby rattle into her pocket, Neil's heart ached for her, and he saw her hands tremble as she picked up a sewing basket and took out an unfinished pillow cover.

"This was hers...my aunt's." She raised pained eyes to Neil. "I'm going to finish it for her."

"Good idea." Neil knew she needed some closure on the loss of her real aunt.

Courtney saw something under the embroidery floss at the bottom of the basket, and when she drew it out, she stared at it as if mesmerized.

"What is it?" Neil asked, peering over her shoulder. "A photo?"

An attractive redheaded woman had her hand on the shoulder of a blond little girl as they stood together smiling at the camera. A merry-go-round was in the background, and the little girl held a bag of pink cotton candy.

"She took me to the carnival. I was six years old. She was ready to love me and my baby, wasn't she?" Courtney's lips quivered. "She must have brought this picture to show me."

"Maybe that's why we came back today," Neil said softly, as he put his arm around her waist. "She wanted you to find it so you would know her invitation was deeply sincere and loving."

They walked out of the houseboat arm in arm, and slammed the door of *Nevermore*. He had just finished loading Courtney's car when his cell phone rang. His expression changed into one of explosive excitement.

"What? We'll be right there."

Courtney's heart was suddenly drumming so loudly she could hear it in her own ears. "What is it?"

"They found the van. Only a few miles from here."

"And?" Her voice choked.

He shook his head. "It's empty, but it may tell us something."

The deserted property in a narrow mountain canyon was about two miles above the lake highway. Neil would have never found it without McGrady's directions. A rutted side road led to a tumbledown cabin that was set back in some trees and hidden from the road. As they approached it, they could see McGrady's car parked in the narrow passage between encroaching shrubs and trees.

"Why…why would she leave it here?" Courtney asked with lips white with fear. Every horrible scenario Courtney had ever heard about kidnappers filled her mind. She had abandoned the van! What did that mean?

God only knows, thought Neil, as he grabbed her hand and they raced down the road.

McGrady and another man stood in front of a dilapidated corral. The gray van was visible parked behind a nearly collapsed log structure. McGrady took one look at Courtney's ashen face and quickly began to explain the situation.

"I just need a definite identification of the van. The license plates are missing. No records in the glove compartment."

"That's it," Neil assured him, saving Courtney's need to answer.

A middle-aged man, dressed like a working cowboy, nodded at Courtney and held out a callused hand to Neil. "I'm Bill Hanks."

"Bill found it," McGrady said.

"Sure did." The man's weathered face creased with a smile. "Sometimes I take a horseback ride down this way. I like to check on the fence which borders my property. Didn't know the police were looking for the van when I called it in." He shook his head. "You have to be careful or some people will make a junkyard any place they can get away with it."

"Any idea how long it's been parked there?" McGrady asked.

"'Fraid not. Let's see, more than a month since I checked the fence, I reckon. Sorry." He sent Courtney an apologetic look. "I just thought someone had dumped it here. Didn't even check to see if the thing would run."

"Does it?" Neil asked.

McGrady nodded. "Got a half tank of gas, too."

"Then why would she abandon it here?" Neil prodded.

"Been asking myself the same question." He scratched his head. He motioned for them to follow him. "See how that underbrush over there is squashed down?" He pointed to a wooded area just beyond the van.

Neil and Courtney started to walk closer to it, but McGrady stopped them with a warning hand. "If she parked the van over there first, that might account for the way the ground has been disturbed. The puzzle is why she'd bother to move it where it is now."

"Don't make much sense," Bill offered.

"You're right. What makes more sense is that she had another vehicle parked over there, waiting."

"And she made a switch," Neil finished.

Courtney's face paled, and he knew what she was thinking.

Now they had no idea what she was driving.

"Of course, we'll be checking with all the car dealers." The detective eyed Courtney speculatively. "I don't suppose she ever mentioned anything that might give us a clue where she was shopping for a vehicle?"

"No, she never told me where she went. Sometimes she was gone nearly the whole day without bringing anything back."

"Obviously some of that time was spent casing the best bank for the robbery. After that, she had to be finalizing her getaway."

"Courtney's decision to leave all of a sudden must have pushed her into speeding things up," Neil speculated.

"Courtney, you told us the gray van was parked in the lot when you decided to sunbathe," McGrady reminded her. "And it was gone both times when you came back to the houseboat, Neil?"

He nodded. "She must have loaded up and left when she thought the ladder accident had taken care of Courtney."

"And probably drove straight here to make the switch," McGrady said.

"So she was already in another car even before the all-points bulletin went out that same night, dammit," Neil swore.

"Looks that way," McGrady agreed. "She must have used money from the bank robbery to purchase another vehicle. My guess is she left the van in some public place while she took possession of her new wheels, and then hunted around for a place to hide it until she was ready to make a switch."

"And she chose this abandoned property," Bill offered, his eyes sparkling with this unexpected drama nearly at his front door.

"She parked her new purchase here, and walked the two miles back to the highway. Resourceful as Billie Kessel is, she probably managed to catch a ride into town to pick up the van."

"Then she drove back to the houseboat without giving Courtney any hint about what was going on."

"Right," McGrady agreed. "The woman was ready to take off as soon as she thought—"

Courtney didn't have to hear any more. She turned away abruptly. With her head down, her fists clenched, she walked away from the men. She was filled with such an overpowering rage that she wanted to throw back her head and scream as loudly as she could.

She heard Neil call her name but she ignored him. She didn't even look back as she angrily thrust her way through thick shrubs and over rocky ground. The pent-up fury that had swelled within her needed release.

She reached down and picked up handfuls of rocks. As if the woman she hated was the target, she hurled them with bitter vengeance. She'd mistaken the woman's diabolical cleverness as harmless eccentricity. If only she had guessed! For the first time in her life, she visualized the power of a gun in her hand.

"Hey, it's me." Neil waved his hand as he came through a nearby stand of spruce trees not far from where the rocks were falling. She'd bolted so quickly out of sight, he'd had trouble finding her.

She dropped the rocks she was holding, and covered her face with her hands to muffle the screams crowding in her throat. Her shoulders visibly shook as he put his arms around her. Anxiety and worry had demanded a release.

"It's okay. Let it all out."

He understood her rage. The devious cleverness of the woman brought bile up in his own throat. He eased her down onto a nearby log, and kept his arm around her until her choked cries gradually weakened.

When her anger was finally spent, she leaned weakly against him. "I guess I lost it," she whispered in a shaky voice.

"After what you've been through, it's long overdue," he assured her as he gently wiped away the beaded sweat on her forehead.

She swallowed hard. "Until now I didn't realize how systematically she arranged everything."

"It's obvious from her rap sheet, she's had practice covering her tracks. But remember, even the best of criminals make mistakes."

How soon? Even one more day was an eternity without Jamie. The only thing that kept her sane was the belief that her baby was getting good care from the woman who had shown such possessive love for him.

"McGrady will find her and return Jamie to you safe and sound," he said firmly, knowing he was trying to convince himself, as well. "And, remember, there are lots of people who are here for you. We could have a houseful anytime you want. My family is just waiting for a green light to descend upon you."

She touched his face. "You're the only one I need."

As she leaned into him, pressing her soft breasts against his chest, she kissed him. He was startled when her lips formed to accept his in an inviting, heated way. His tongue teased the corner of her mouth, and desire shot through him as she willingly accepted it.

As their kisses deepened, he wanted to mold her supple body with his hands until the spiraling hunger between them was satisfied. Only the fear of adding to her emotional trauma stopped him. She was not in command of herself. Her great need had made her vulnerable, and he feared she was just inviting a momentary escape.

He lifted his mouth from her soft pliable lips, and his voice was unsteady. "We'd better get back. McGrady will wonder what happened to us."

As he drew her to her feet, she was reeling slightly from the spiral of heated passion that had flared between them. Neither of them spoke as he guided her through the wooded area and back to where the van had been found.

McGrady regarded Courtney uneasily. "Sorry to put you through this."

"It's all right. I just had to vent a little." She avoided looking at Neil.

While they had been gone, two more men had arrived in another police car. They circled the gray van and carefully examined the ground in the immediate area.

"What are they doing?" she asked.

"Comparing the van's tire tread to the faint impressions left where another vehicle might have been parked."

"Can they tell what kind?" Neil prodded.

McGrady just shrugged. "There's no need for you two to hang around any longer. I know this can't be easy for you, Courtney."

"You'll call me if—"

"If we have any new developments," he finished for her. "Now try to get some rest. Go home."

Home? She stared at him as if the simple word had absolutely no meaning for her.

"That's a good idea," Neil said quickly.

They drove back to the lake highway in silence, and he kept glancing at her. He didn't know what to expect next, but he sure as hell wasn't going to let her out of his sight, if he could help it. They had loaded her belongings into his car, but hers remained parked in the area above the houseboat.

"I'll have someone bring your car up to the house."

Courtney knew from Neil's firm tone that he expected an argument, but the car could stay there until it rusted as far as she was concerned. She'd never be able to force herself to go anywhere near that abominable houseboat again. Even now, its insidious evil reached out to her.

When Neil pulled into the driveway of his house, he turned off the engine and sat with his hands grasping the steering wheel. Then he turned and looked at her.

"I don't know how to say this without causing you offense." He took a deep breath. "You already know that I've had overnight female guests in my house. But I've always protected my privacy, and I've never, ever invited a woman to move in with me. Even if the circumstances were different, you would be the first, Courtney." His eyes searched her face. "I want you to think of making this your home, you and Jamie, without any commitment or strings attached. Do you hear what I'm saying?"

She moistened her dry lips, struggling to accept his offer without compromising herself or him. "I don't know what to say."

"It's easy. You could say something like, I'd be delighted, Mr. Ellsworth. I accept your offer, Mr. Ellsworth. Or anything else that comes to mind."

A faint smile reached her eyes. "How about, yes, Mr. Ellsworth."

Chapter Twelve

The next few days settled into a predictable routine. Every morning, Courtney had a simple breakfast ready when Neil came down to the kitchen.

"How'd you sleep?" he asked even though the dark circles under her eyes were answer enough.

"Better," she lied, not admitting she fought to stay awake because of nightmares that tormented her. Sometimes when she was caught in an exhausted slumber, she'd hear Jamie's cry and be on her feet instantly, saying, "I'm coming, honey." Then cold reality would hit her and send her shivering back to bed.

Other times, she'd be jerked awake by a remembered movement of the houseboat, and her nostrils would quiver with rank waterlogged smells. She'd lie awake for hours, only falling asleep when utter exhaustion overtook her.

"Why don't you relax on the patio this morning while I make a quick trip to the office? Unless you'd like to come with me?" Neil asked one morning.

She shook her head. "No, I'll be fine. I'd rather stay here."

Neil had arranged for someone from his brothers' garage to deliver her car. She had the freedom to come and go as she wished, but she never left the house.

She wasn't sleeping well, he knew, and he had been fighting a nightly battle to stay in his own room. He longed to hold her, comfort her and make love to her, but he'd promised her no strings, no commitments. He waited for some sign that she welcomed the heated passion that they had shared in the woods.

He postponed his housekeeper's regular visit at Courtney's insistence. He didn't argue because he could tell she needed some physical activity to keep her busy.

"Don't overdo," he warned as he prepared to leave. "You have my office number. Don't hesitate to call—for any reason."

"I'll be fine."

He kissed her lightly on the cheek, resisting the temptation to take her into his arms and forget about going anywhere. Never would he have believed he was capable of the willpower he'd shown since Courtney moved in with him.

"I'll get back as early as I can. Again, don't be afraid to call anytime—about anything."

The lovely house was empty without him. Courtney listlessly wandered from one room to the other. Every time the phone rang, she jumped. McGrady had been successful in limiting news coverage after the story first broke. After a couple of reporters were denied interviews with Courtney, local interest had shifted to other stories.

The detective was good about calling and keeping Courtney up to date on the investigation. McGrady softened all his negative reports with a promise that things would be turning around soon.

"We've circulated a description of Billie Kessel to all the used and new car dealers in the area. So far we've drawn a blank, but that doesn't mean anything. I've got people checking on recent newspaper ads. If anyone has sold a vehicle to someone matching her description, we'll check it out," he had promised her.

After Neil had gone, and Courtney was finishing cleaning up the kitchen, the doorbell rang. She was surprised to see Alex, one of the twins, smiling at her when she opened the door.

"Hi, did I miss Neil?"

"I'm afraid so. He left for the office about an hour ago."

She'd only met Alex once, at the family gathering, but she remembered his smile, and the affectionate way he treated his wife, Hollie.

"Oh, I thought he was working at home..." He looked a little embarrassed.

"Yes, he has been," Courtney assured him, adding with a wry smile, "I think I finally convinced him that I don't need a babysitter."

"I'm really sorry...about what's happened," he told her with obvious sincerity. "We all are."

"Thank you. Won't you come in?"

"Maybe for a minute. Something came to mind this morning when I was talking to my wife, Hollie, about a car I sold yesterday. It probably doesn't mean anything." He hesitated as if he shouldn't be saying anything to Courtney. "I thought I'd just run it by Neil and he could decide if we should pass it on to McGrady."

Courtney ushered him into the living room. After motioning him toward the sofa, she sat down in a chair facing him, and leaned forward expectantly. "What is it?"

"It may be nothing," he answered quickly, obviously reacting to her intensity. "The police put out a bulletin asking us to report any sale to a woman matching that woman's description."

"Yes, I know." Her heart missed a beat. "And you sold a car to someone like that?"

"No," he answered quickly. "I would have immediately called the police if that had been the case."

She knew her face visibly fell, but she couldn't help it. "Oh, I thought maybe—"

"I'm sorry. Maybe I'm way off base even giving any thought to what happened yesterday." He suddenly seemed embarrassed to be even talking about it. "It's just that I got to talking to a retired couple who were waiting to sign papers on a new car. You know my brother and I own the Ellsworth Motor Company?"

"Yes, I do," she answered quickly, impatient for him to get to the reason for his visit.

"Well, in the course of conversation the man mentioned getting rid of their used vehicle by parking it in their yard and putting a For Sale sign on it. They were surprised when a lone woman came by and bought it without any hesitation."

"And the woman fit the description?" she asked eagerly.

"I have no idea. I just thought I should mention it to Neil and he could check it out."

Her heart sank as quickly as it had risen. In a town as large as Manitou, and the adjoining areas, the incident of one woman buying a used car wouldn't mean a thing. Such sales probably happened a hundred times every day.

Alex must have seen her face fall because he added quickly, "The thing that struck me was the fact they wanted seven thousand dollars for it, and she paid cash."

NEIL HAD JUST STARTED to make headway on the pile of documents on his desk when his brother and Courtney burst into the office.

"Alex needs to talk to you."

He couldn't believe his eyes. When he'd left the house, Courtney's expression had been lifeless and pale. Now there was color in her cheeks, and her eyes were alive with excitement. His brother Alex was obviously involved.

"What on earth is going on with you two?"

"Tell him, Alex," Courtney urged. Her look warned that if he didn't do it quickly, she would.

"It may be nothing," Alex began. "But then again…"

Neil listened intently as his brother told him the same story he'd told Courtney.

"It didn't hit me until this morning that a woman paying cash was damn unusual. I mean, how many people go around with seven thousand dollars in their pocket?"

Neil's own heartbeat began to quicken. "Did they describe the woman?"

He shook his head. "They just mentioned in passing that they'd sold their secondhand vehicle for cash to a woman who'd seen their For Sale sign in the yard. I guess the quickness of the sale totally surprised them. Anyway, I thought maybe you'd want to check it out."

"Alex can give us the name and address," Courtney said eagerly. "We can check it out."

"I think we'd better call McGrady, first. We ought to get his input before we do anything." Neil reached for the phone and quickly dialed the number.

Courtney waited nervously. She knew she shouldn't get her hopes up about something that could turn out to be a bust, but she couldn't help it. Following up on even a flimsy lead like this was better than being alone, anxiously waiting for the telephone to ring.

When Neil finally got through the switchboard to McGrady's secretary, he was told that the detective was "in the field."

"No, I don't think he can be contacted at the moment, Mr. Ellsworth, unless it's a dire emergency."

Neil had no choice but to leave a message asking McGrady to contact him.

"How soon will he be back in the office?" Courtney asked anxiously.

"His secretary couldn't say."

Courtney was not agreeable to waiting one minute longer to check out the lead, McGrady or no McGrady. She argued, "I don't see any harm in talking to the couple. The police can follow up if we discover anything."

The determined set of her chin warned Neil she was going to follow through on this lead, with or without his approval. He couldn't blame her. In the same situation, he'd probably do the same.

"All right," he agreed. "We'll go have a talk with them, but we have to be careful not to jump to a lot of conclusions. McGrady will be furious if we muddy the waters and make his job harder."

Neil would have preferred to check out the possible lead himself. It would have been better if Alex had come straight to him. Raising Courtney's hopes, only to have them crash, wasn't going to help a bit.

"I'll get the name and address for you," Alex volunteered, and quickly called his office. He wrote down the information and handed Neil the slip of paper. "I'll let you take it from here. I'm booked up with possible clients this morning, and Allen will have my scalp if I don't show."

"Thank you for your help," Courtney told him.

He crossed his fingers. "Let me know."

Courtney's stomach was filled with butterflies as they drove to the address Alex had given them. It was located in a suburban housing development for moderate-income families, and the one belonging to Gladys and Frank O'Brian was a well-kept ranch house with a new SUV parked in the driveway.

Courtney looked at Neil for encouragement as they walked up the walk to the front door, but his expression was unreadable. She couldn't tell whether he was deciding how to handle the situation, or regretting he hadn't insisted on leaving the investigation in McGrady's hands. At the moment, she really didn't care. She stood stiffly beside him as they waited for someone to answer the doorbell.

After a couple of minutes, a husky man with cropped gray hair opened the door.

"Yes?" His expression was both friendly and guarded.

"Mr. Frank O'Brian?"

"Yep, that's me."

As Neil quickly introduced himself and Courtney, the man's expression changed to one of puzzlement. "Are you selling something?"

"No," Neil readily assured him. "We'd like to talk to you about a vehicle you had for sale."

"Too late," he said, smiling broadly. "We sold it a couple of weeks ago. A nice quick sale, it was, too."

"Yes, we know. It's the buyer we're interested in. If you could spare a few minutes to tell us about her, we'd certainly appreciate it," Neil said smoothly.

"Don't know if I can tell you much, but come on in. It's too damn hot to stand out there." As he stepped back from the door and motioned them into a small but pleasant living room, he yelled, "Gladys!"

A tiny gray-haired woman wearing bright pink capri pants and a baggy top bustled in from the kitchen. She had a puzzled look on her pleasant face when she saw Courtney and Neil standing there.

"Sorry to bother you," Neil said quickly. "We're

trying to identify the woman who bought your vehicle, and wonder if you and your husband might help us?"

"You want her name?"

"Yes, that would help," Neil assured her.

"It was a real common one, wasn't it, Frank? Jane Smith."

"She gave us a P.O. box address," he added.

"Could you describe her for us?" Courtney asked. "Did she have red hair?"

"Couldn't rightly say. She wore one of those handkerchiefs pulled back from her forehead and tied in the back. Couldn't see her hair."

"What about her build. Tall, short, thin, fat?"

"Taller than me," the woman answered, chuckling. "'Course, everybody past the sixth grade can say that."

"You're a peewee, all right," Frank said kindly. "I reckon this gal was average height, and about one hundred and twenty pounds."

"Just ordinary looking, I'd say," his wife remarked.

"And she paid cash for your used car?"

Frank frowned. "Oh, we didn't have a car for sale."

"She bought our used camper," his wife added.

"You sold her a camper?" Neil repeated, avoiding the crushed expression on Courtney's face.

Camper? How likely was it Billie would buy a camper when she needed a quick getaway?

"Yep. Had a lot of miles on it. That's why we could let it go cheap. But in good condition," Frank insisted. "I had a mechanic look the camper over."

Courtney sat down on a rather lumpy couch and struggled to come to terms with a bitter disappointment.

Neil's cell phone sounded and he apologized as he answered it. She knew it must be McGrady when Neil quickly explained where they were and gave the address.

After he hung up, Neil advised the O'Brians that Detective McGrady was on his way to speak with them. Gladys moved closer to her husband and Frank's accommodating manner disappeared.

"What is this all about?" he demanded, openly on the defensive. "We didn't do anything wrong. That camper was ours. We had the right to sell it to anybody that came along."

"Easy, Frank," soothed his wife, touched his sleeve. "Let them explain."

Her husband wasn't that easily pacified. "Why you bringing the police into this? We're law-abiding citizens. Never had any dealings with the police except for a couple of damn parking tickets."

"Please." Courtney held up her hand to stop the tirade. "We're trying to find the woman who stole my baby."

A grenade thrown in the middle of the living-room floor couldn't have been any more effective in creating a stunned silence. Both Frank and Gladys just stared at her.

She swallowed hard as if the words were burrs in her throat. "A woman posing as my aunt took my four-month-old son. She drove a gray van and we found it abandoned."

"We know she had money for another vehicle," Neil added quickly. "And when you told my brother that your buyer paid cash for your used vehicle, we had to check it out. Unfortunately we thought it was a car or truck that you'd sold. We wouldn't have bothered you otherwise."

"Oh, honey, I'm so sorry." Gladys hurried to sit down beside Courtney. "We don't read the papers, or even watch much TV. Too much violence."

"We'll try to help all we can," Frank promised, his irritation completely disappeared.

When McGrady arrived, Neil could tell he wasn't pleased that they hadn't waited for him to make contact with the O'Brians in the first place.

"We don't want to impose upon you folks," he said in his homey way. "We'd appreciate any information you can give us to clear this thing up."

"I don't know why a kidnapper would want to buy a used camper," Frank spoke up. "You don't have much speed, takes a lot more gas. Doesn't make sense."

"Not the smartest thing to buy when you're trying to make a getaway," McGrady agreed.

"Unless you don't think like other people," Neil offered thoughtfully. "Maybe that's why this Jane Smith buyer could be Billie Mae. God knows, her mind runs on a different track."

"We can clear all of this up once we verify the woman's identification," McGrady said flatly.

"We want to help," Gladys assured him. "Don't we, Frank?"

Her husband nodded dutifully.

"Okay, we have a name and a P.O. box. If that doesn't check out, even the smallest memory you have about this woman could help us identify her. Do you still have any of the bills she gave you?" McGrady inquired in his usual affable way.

Frank shook his head. "No, we deposited the seven thousand right away. We didn't want that kind of money lying around the house. Why?"

"There's a chance we might have gotten her fingerprint off the money. Did she touch anything else while she was here?" He looked hopefully at Gladys as if the woman might have used the bathroom.

Gladys shook her head. "She didn't even come in the house. Frank took care of the sale in the driveway where the camper was parked."

"Did she take possession of the camper the day she bought it?"

Frank nodded. "Drove it right off."

"What about the car she arrived in?"

He frowned. "I remember her saying she saw my sign when she was driving by earlier. I just assumed that she lived somewhere in the development and had walked here to see about buying the camper."

"The bus stops up at the corner," Gladys said. "Maybe that's how she got here."

"Come to think of it, she did seem in kind of a hurry to take possession. It's a good thing we had the camper cleaned out and ready to go."

"Wait a minute!" Gladys's eyes lit up. "I remembered something. I'd been cleaning the windows, and left a bottle of glass cleaner on the dashboard. When she got ready to drive off, she handed it to me."

"Good girl," McGrady said. "Was she wearing gloves?" When Gladys shook her head, he smiled. "I'd like to take that bottle down to the lab, and see what we can find. Will you carefully put it in a sack for me?"

Courtney's emotions had been a Ferris wheel, rising and falling as she listened to the conversation. Her hopes had been dashed when they had learned the woman had bought a camper, and had risen again when Neil had insisted that it was something the deranged Billie Mae would do.

"Well, thanks for your time, folks," McGrady said as he prepared to leave. "We appreciate your cooperation."

"You'll let us know what you find out, won't you?" Gladys asked as she handed him a plastic bag. "I won't be able to rest until I know whether or not that horrible woman is the one who is using our camper."

McGrady promised to let them know the results of the fingerprinting analysis as soon as he knew anything. He walked out to the car with Neil and Courtney.

"We should be able to tell in quick order if we've got a match with Kessel's fingerprints. I can't put out an APB on the camper until I know for sure that Billie Mae Kessel was the buyer."

"What about license plates?"

"Frank said they left theirs on the camper, but that doesn't mean anything. Billie's smart enough to put on bogus plates that will pass superficial scrutiny."

"Every day counts," Courtney said in a tight voice.

"I know, honey." He patted her shoulder. "We'll move as fast as we can, I promise. If I can get forensic on the ball, we may have the results before the day is over."

Neil headed home instead of back to the office. His former skepticism had vanished, but he knew better than to admit it to Courtney at this point. He could tell she was struggling to keep a tight rein on her emotions. Every development seemed to be a cliff-hanger.

He didn't want to leave Courtney alone, so as soon as they got home, he telephoned Maribeth. "I've got to get back to the office. Courtney needs some company while she waits for a telephone call. I'll let her tell you about it."

At first Courtney was irritated by Neil's insistence that she shouldn't be alone, but it turned out that Maribeth's company was a blessing. Courtney couldn't help but respond to the woman's upbeat, supportive presence.

"Okay, tell me all. What's going on?"

Gratefully, Courtney told her about Alex's visit, and the result of their visit and conversation with the O'Brians.

"How wonderful. You have Kessel's fingerprints?"

"We don't know. McGrady's going to call me."

When the phone rang midafternoon, Courtney's hand trembled as she lifted the receiver.

"We've got a match," McGrady told her. "I'll keep in touch."

When she hung up, Maribeth searched her face. "Is it good, or bad news?"

"I don't know," she answered as her thoughts raced.

A camper was a moveable house. It could be parked anywhere. How would they ever find it?

Chapter Thirteen

When Neil came home at dusk, Maribeth's car was gone and no lights were on in the house. Late-afternoon shadows enveloped the hall, living room and den. A sense of emptiness warned him he'd become much too accustomed to Courtney's presence in the house.

He turned on lights and then bounded up the stairs. She's probably taking a nap, he thought, as he quietly made his way to the guest suite. Peering in the darkened room, he saw the bed was empty and there was no sign of her sitting listlessly in a chair in front of the window as she had been prone to do.

She must have gone home with Maribeth, he decided as he made his way back downstairs. He'd never had trouble filling up his time at home before. Even though his housekeeper was efficient, there were still chores he liked to do. Spending a few minutes watering the plants on the patio usually cleared his head from long days at the office.

Sometimes he waited until twilight before he raided the fridge for the meal the housekeeper had left for him. Contrary to his reputation as a man-about-town, he enjoyed an evening of solitude.

But not tonight.

As he crossed the hall to the kitchen, a faint sound of gurgling water reached his ears. Turning in that direction, he saw a sliver of light under the door leading to the Jacuzzi. He was surprised at the wave of relief that swept over him when he saw Courtney sitting in the hot tub.

"So there you are. I've been all over the house looking for you," he chided. "I thought, maybe, you'd gone home with Maribeth."

"She left a little while ago."

He frowned. "What was her hurry?"

"She has a family to look after," Courtney reminded him. "Your sister is good company, and I appreciate her spending time with me, but I can handle being alone."

"I would have left the office earlier, but I got caught up in the fallout of that business with Delaney and Woodword."

"What's happening?"

"The district attorney is getting ready to go to trial." He set his jaw. "I had to provide a lot of the financial details that will convict them. It'll be a relief when all that's settled once and for all."

"You look tired."

"It's been some day, hasn't it?"

"Would you like to join me?"

He hesitated, remembering the passionate fire that had ignited when they'd been in the Jacuzzi together. He wasn't at all sure that he could keep his hands off her luscious body. He thought about her almost constantly, and it was becoming harder all the time to keep his distance.

"Please."

The invitation in her soft eyes reassured him and he nodded in acceptance. "Be with you in a minute."

As Courtney waited for Neil to change, she leaned her head back against the edge of the tub, closed her eyes and remembered the conversation she'd had with Maribeth that afternoon.

They had sat at the small round table in the kitchen, having coffee and sharing the challenges of keeping their lives on an even keel. Courtney had never shared with anyone the disappointments in her marriage.

"I never had any real companionship with Clyde. When he wasn't working, he was off somewhere, drinking beer, watching football or playing poker with the boys. When I became a widow, I decided I didn't want another man complicating my life." She looked steadily at Maribeth. "I haven't done a lot of dating because I've chosen to go it alone. I think I made the right decision."

Maribeth studied Courtney over the rim of her coffee mug. Then, clearing her throat, she said, "I suppose I should be staying out of this. But, you know, fools rush in. May I say something?"

"Please."

"I don't want my brother hurt," she said in a forthright manner. "For the first time since Wendy, Neil's really opened himself up and allowed himself to care. Do you hear what I'm saying?"

"I think so," Courtney replied hesitantly.

"For years, he's tried to cover up his deep sensitivity, but you've really gotten to him. Just look at him! He's got dark circles under his eyes. He's lost that jaunty step of his. He'll do anything in the world for you, even take on your pain if he could."

How could she put into words what Neil's support had meant to her? "I don't know what I would do without him. He's been my only anchor."

Maribeth covered Courtney's hand with her own. "Heaven knows, you're trying to handle a myriad of torturous feelings right now. I can't even imagine what you're going through," she admitted. "The thing is, I'm worried that the fallout from all this may leave my brother deeply wounded again."

"I wouldn't willingly hurt Neil, ever. You have to believe me."

Maribeth looked at her with those knowing eyes. "I think you're so afraid of being hurt that you're turning a blind eye to the love he's offering you. You're trying to protect yourself at his expense."

"I don't know what you mean."

"Of course you do. You're willing to deny your own feelings because you lack the courage to accept them," Maribeth said bluntly. "That's not fair to Neil, nor to you."

As Courtney played the conversation over in her mind, she realized Neil's sister had seen her for the coward she was. Instead of wanting a guarantee for a nebulous future, she should be reaching out with both hands to this man who had captured her heart. Life was too fragile to throw a moment of it away.

When Neil slipped into the water beside her, Courtney sent a playful handful of water spraying in his face.

He was so surprised that he laughed out loud and did a double take. Her eyes were shining and her lips parted in a challenging grin. He quickly rallied and sent a swish of water back at her.

Like two boisterous kids, they gave themselves up to childish play and released pent-up pressures that had been building within them.

"Take that!"

"And that!"

When Courtney's hair was soaked and she was blinded by water streaming down her face, she laughingly blubbered, "I give up."

Neil willingly accepted her surrender. Droplets of water glistened on her long lashes, and wet fair hair clung to her lovely cheeks and forehead. Just looking at her stirred desires in a way he wouldn't have thought possible. He felt a mounting need to claim every part of her.

Neil's eyes held a dreamy look that Courtney had never seen before. It made her aware of how little she really knew about this man who had given her so much. Maribeth had been right about a lot of things. The present moment was all they really had, and because of her self-protective attitude, she'd been ready to cheat both of them of it.

"You look as if you want to kiss me," she said boldly as she put her arms around him.

"Well, you did surrender," he reminded her, not quite sure how to handle her forwardness.

"Yes, I did," she agreed softly. Putting her hand on the back of his neck, she drew his face down to hers.

The sweet, pliable softness of her lips matched the promise in her yielding body. When she breathlessly withdrew from his embrace, he read the promise in her eyes.

Without speaking, they climbed out of the Jacuzzi and made their way to his bedroom. Discarding their wet suits on the floor, they buried themselves under the warm covers of his king-size bed. He drew her moist nakedness against his.

As a floodgate of desire flowed between them, he led her from one exploding crescendo to another. Tenderly and passionately, he heightened their pleasure until an encompassing sensation of bewildering fulfillment exploded between them.

Tears of happiness filled her eyes as they lay together, spent and satiated with lovemaking. As her head rested upon his bare chest, she was aware of his rhythmic breathing and was totally content in the quiet awareness of his nearness.

Maribeth had been right. Courtney had been cheating them both by trying to protect herself from falling in love. Whatever the future, she would have this moment to remember and be strengthened to face whatever lay ahead.

About midnight, they enjoyed a snack that Neil brought up to the bedroom. They talked until about two o'clock, made love again, and then fell asleep. The next morning, they leisurely made their way down to the kitchen for breakfast.

As another day without Jamie faced her, the brief respite Courtney had felt in Neil's arms slowly began to fade.

Another day. Where's my baby!

She couldn't help resting her head in her hand as Neil was getting the coffee. She felt totally helpless and filled with a growing fury. When Neil asked her what she'd like for breakfast, she just shook her head.

"Surprise me."

"All right, I'll make you the specialty of the house." He reached for a waffle mix, and was busily greasing the waffle iron when the doorbell rang.

They both froze and looked at each other.

"I'll get it." Courtney tightened the belt on her silk bathrobe as she hurried down the hall.

When she opened the door and saw McGrady, hope pounded in her chest. He shook his head in answer to her unspoken question, and her stomach made that too-familiar sickening drop.

"Just thought I'd drop by and give you a little update," he said, trying to ease her disappointment. "Am I too early?"

"Not at all."

"Come on in, Detective," Neil said, coming up behind Courtney. "I make a mean cup of coffee, and if you like waffles, you're in luck."

McGrady touched his ample middle. "My wife would kill me if I had a double breakfast, but I'll take the coffee."

They returned to the kitchen and the detective sat down at the table with them.

"What's up?" Neil asked as he poured McGrady

a cup of coffee. He knew the detective hadn't dropped by to chat.

Courtney's impatience flared when McGrady responded in that infuriatingly slow way of his. He took several sips of coffee as if this were some kind of a social call.

"Mmm." He nodded his head approvingly. "I have to agree, Neil. You make damn good coffee."

"You said you had an update?" Courtney prodded, clasping her hands so tightly under the table that her nails bit into her flesh.

McGrady leaned back in his chair and his soft brown eyes surveyed the two of them. "I thought you'd be interested to know we found a bullet embedded in one of the trees where your car went off the road. The lab tested it against the one taken out of Harold Jensen's body."

"And?" Neil prodded.

"They matched. That puts a wrap on my theory that the two crimes were linked," McGrady said in satisfaction. "They both came from the same army revolver, and it's clear that Billie Kessel is our shooter."

"If she uses the gun again, you'll know it, won't you?" Neil asked.

"Possibly. As I told you yesterday, the lab matched the print on the Windex bottle. It was Billie Mae Kessel who bought that camper, all right."

Courtney's stomach turned over hearing the truth once again, and she pushed away her untouched waffle.

"What happens now?" Neil put his arm across the back of her chair and rested his hand on her shoulder.

"Now that we can tie Kessel to a specific vehicle, it may be easier to pick up some information on her whereabouts. I talked to the O'Brians last night and got a detailed description of the camper. We're hoping our national APB will get some results."

"What about the license plates?" Neil asked. "Do you think she'll leave those on the camper?"

"I doubt it. My guess is that she's using some old plates from another car or one she's stolen."

"And what if she abandons the camper for a different kind of transportation—the way she did the gray van?" Courtney swallowed hard. "Then we're back to square one."

McGrady took a long swig of coffee before he answered, "Nobody can play Russian roulette forever. Sooner or later the odds catch up with them."

"That could be years!" Courtney cried. "You hear all the time about that happening. A stolen baby becomes an adult before it's found—if ever. Even if parents pay a huge ransom, they may never get the child back."

"We're not dealing with a kidnapping for money," he reminded her. "And that gives us an advantage. We have more time and more assurance that we'll find your baby unharmed and safe."

Courtney clung to his promise as the next two days crept by without any positive response to the nationwide APB. Nights were a haven of momentary peace in Neil's arms. She was thankful for the strength they shared. It allowed her to handle the constant worry of her missing child.

The long days were the worst. While Neil was at the office, Maribeth loyally kept her company. She managed to keep the conversation flowing, and even read aloud some articles from her favorite women's magazines.

"You don't have to entertain me," Courtney protested. She felt more like crawling into bed and pulling the covers up over her head.

"Let's drive down to the city park," Maribeth proposed. "A good hardy walk will do you good. We can people-watch, buy our lunch from a vendor and soak up the sunshine."

In the end, Courtney found it easier to give in than to argue. After all, it really didn't matter where she was. The same nagging anxiety went with her.

Neil was delighted when Maribeth called and told him where they were going. "Good job, sis. Keep her busy."

Courtney was surprised when Maribeth drove to the same recreational area where she'd been with Neil on their first outing together. The lakeside park was crowded as usual, and Maribeth set a brisk walking pace that challenged Courtney to keep up. Both of them were sweating and breathing heavily when they finished their walk and threw themselves down on the lawn to rest.

"Now it's time for lunch," Maribeth declared. They were on their way to find a hot-dog vendor when she suddenly stopped and pointed ahead. "Isn't that Neil?"

He waved when he caught sight of them.

Courtney's heart caught. What was he doing

there? *Good news? Bad news?* His expression was one of excitement when he reached them.

"Thank God I found you in this crowded place."

"What is it?" Courtney demanded in a strained voice.

"I just got a call at the office from McGrady. He wants us to come to the police station right away."

"What's happening, Neil?" Maribeth demanded excitedly.

"Have they found the camper?" Courtney's voice rose in sudden hope.

"McGrady doesn't know," Neil answered quickly. "A park ranger in Ridgewood State Park called in a report a few minutes ago. A camper fitting the APB description has been parked in one of the campgrounds."

The ground under Courtney's feet suddenly seemed to dip and she clutched Neil for support.

"Oh, my God," Maribeth breathed.

"A single woman has parked it there for a couple of weeks. She doesn't have red hair, but she fits the age and physical description."

"And Jamie?" Courtney's mouth was dry and her pulse thumped loudly in her ears.

"No sign of a baby, but that doesn't mean anything," he assured her. "Billie's smart enough not to go showing him off all over the place."

"I'm sure Jamie's all right, Courtney," Maribeth said quickly. "The woman went to all the trouble to snatch him. Why wouldn't she take good care of him?"

Her words were meant to be reassuring, but they landed heavily on Courtney's heart. There was no assurance that the woman's behavior would remain consistent.

"McGrady wants us to ride with him so we can make a positive identification of the woman, one way or the other."

"I'll be waiting to hear," Maribeth called after them as they hurried to his car.

Neil glanced at Courtney's ashen face as they pulled into the police station. "Maybe it would be better if I went with the detective, and you stayed here. I can make the identification as easily as you. No need to put you through this, if the woman isn't Kessel."

Courtney firmed her chin. "I'm not going to sit around here, waiting to find out. If I can put my arms around Jamie one minute sooner by going, I'm going to do it."

McGrady was waiting for them. "Have you explained the situation to her, Neil?"

He nodded. "There's a report of a woman with a camper like the O'Brians parked in a campground."

"Right. But you have to remember, thousands of those campers were sold all over the country. There's no assurance this is the one we're looking for. We don't have an updated photo of Billie Kessel, and her general description could fit any number of women her age. That's why I want you two to come along with Officer Rogers and me. Are you up to it, Courtney?"

"Yes," she answered readily. "I want to be there just in case…" Her voice trailed off.

"You'll both do exactly what I tell you. No arguments. Until we assess the situation, you two will remain out of sight."

"Yes, sir," Neil answered, but Courtney remained silent. Adrenaline was pouring through her at such a rate she wanted to do something besides hold her hands and wait.

"This could take a matter of minutes, or hours," McGrady warned. "We may be able to walk up to the woman and learn in short order who she is, but the worst scenario would be if we have to do a stakeout."

Dear God, no. "If that happens no telling what danger Jamie might be in," Courtney said.

McGrady avoided acknowledging her. "I'll try to keep you posted on what's happening. If it's a false alarm, we'll know soon enough."

False alarm!

Neil kept his arm around Courtney's waist. "But if it is Kessel?"

"She won't get away," McGrady promised. "We'll have units at every exit of the park."

An unbidden horror stabbed Courtney. "What if she tries to run, and holds Jamie as a hostage?"

"We'll deal with it," he answered flatly.

A few minutes later Courtney and Neil sat in the back seat of a police cruiser as it raced toward Ridgeway State Park a hundred miles way.

Chapter Fourteen

Under different circumstances, Courtney might have found riding in a police cruiser an exciting experience, but its wailing siren, high speed and constant radio monitor blended into a pulse-racing roar in her head.

Seated in the front passenger's seat, McGrady's usually relaxed body language was missing. A tight muscle flickered in his jaw, his broad neck was stiff and his shoulders tense. She couldn't hear what he said in low tones to Rogers, the plainclothes policeman who was driving.

With siren blaring, the police car made its way in and out of city traffic. When they left Manitou's city limits behind, traffic thinned on a four-lane highway heading east into a high range of mountains. A few times McGrady turned around and flashed her a reassuring smile that failed to soften the sober glint in his eyes.

As Courtney sat there, staring unseeingly ahead, her heart was in her throat. As the miles swept by, she was glad that Neil didn't try to fill the silence with empty words. The way his hand gripped hers betrayed his own inner stress, but his presence was a steadying force.

As she stared out the window, a view of dark encroaching mountains whizzed past at a dizzying rate. As they drew closer and closer to the state park, Courtney knew she had to prepare herself for either a heartrending disappointment, or an ugly encounter with the wily, unscrupulous woman who had pretended to be her aunt.

"I'm scared," she whispered, tightening her grip on Neil's hand.

Neil brushed her cheek with his lips. "Honey, you'll handle it. Whatever happens, you'll come through it with courage. And I'll be with you every step of the way."

The police car slowed its speed and turned off the highway. They could see some buildings, an archway made of peeled logs and a large sign, Ridgewood State Park.

"The campground is about ten miles ahead," Neil told her quickly when he saw the spurt of fright in her eyes. "Those buildings are the lodge, gift shop and café. We used to come up here quite a bit when I was a kid. You know, Boy Scouts. Family outings and the like."

Two state-trooper cars were parked just beyond the sign, and uniformed officers were checking vehicles waiting to leave the park. McGrady gave an identifying wave, and one of the highway patrolmen came quickly over to the cruiser's window.

McGrady greeted him by name. "Fill me in, Tom. What's the setup?"

"We've got two patrolmen stationed at both of the park's exits. Nobody driving is getting through the road blocks without clearance," the officer assured him. "We responded as soon as we were notified, and so far, no woman close to the description has tried to come through."

"Good," McGrady said. "We'll let you know whether we need more backup."

"The forest ranger who made the call is waiting for you right outside the campground, and we have another unit on alert," the patrolman told him.

"Thank you, Sergeant. We'll assess the situation, and let you know."

The officer glanced in the back at Courtney and tipped his hat as if to assure her that he was on her side.

"All right, let's get on with it." McGrady nodded at the driver.

Courtney pulled back into the shadows of the back seat as their police cruiser passed a line of halted cars waiting to leave the park. She could see people staring out their windows with expressions of irritation and curiosity.

Neil was thankful that the press hadn't gotten wind of what was going on and showed up with their cameras running. He hoped the police had orders not to admit them to the park. Courtney didn't need that kind of hassle.

"Looks like they've got everything under control," he assured her in a low voice.

She nodded, but didn't believe it for a minute. Someone as resourceful as Billie Mae Kessel wouldn't be stupid enough to drive up to a police road block and expect to get through. As cunning as she was, it was impossible to predict what her twisted mind might conceive, especially if the pressure was on.

Thick stands of conifer trees boxed in the two-lane road leading into the heart of the state park. Occasionally, a narrow dirt road identified with a poetic name like Harmony or Meadowlark wound its way into a tunnel of trees, and Neil realized how difficult it would be to find someone hiding in the concealing thickness of trees and undergrowth.

If Billie Mae decided to run—

He shoved the thought away and kept his eyes lowered, fearing Courtney might read his thoughts.

"The ranger station is just ahead at the entrance to the campground," McGrady said, looking back at Courtney. When a tremor passed her lips, his eyes shifted to Neil. "I'm depending on you, Neil. She many need some looking after."

"I'm your man," Neil assured him.

The station stood just inside the entrance to the main campground, and a park ranger was waiting on the porch. He came quickly down the steps as the police cruiser pulled to a stop and McGrady got out.

"I'm Ranger Bob Lewis," he said, identifying himself.

"You're the one who made the call?" McGrady asked.

"Yes, sir. I've been off for ten days, and only read the APB this morning," the ranger explained. "I noticed the woman this morning when was she coming out of the laundry building. When I said hello and asked her a couple of innocent questions about how long she'd be staying, her reaction was so defensive it caught my attention. If it hadn't been for the APB, I would have probably shrugged it off."

"I'm certainly glad you didn't," McGrady told him. "We want to follow up on every possible lead."

"I'm sorry the other ranger isn't here. He was called up to the lake last night because of some emergency, and I'm not sure when he'll be back. That makes us one man short."

"We've got manpower in reserve, if we need it. First of all, we have to find out what we're dealing with here."

"Yes, sir."

McGrady motioned for Courtney and Neil to follow him. "You two can stay inside the station while we check things out." His tone softened as he looked at Courtney. "You going to be okay?"

Not trusting her voice to answer him, she just nodded. How could she know whether she would be "okay"? It was all she could do to maintain a semblance of normality when her insides were churning and her skin was clammy with nervous sweat.

"We'll have to take it slow and sure," McGrady warned her. "If we're dealing with Billie, we don't want to light any kind of a fuse in that crazy head of hers. Right?"

Courtney managed to echo, "Right," even though she wondered how she could possibly handle the wait. She knew better than anyone how devious and ruthless the woman could be.

"We trust your judgment," Neil assured him as they mounted the front steps and entered the wooden rectangular building.

The inside of the ranger station was strictly government issue. The furniture was serviceable, the walls painted a sandy beige, and had very few personal effects of the two men who lived there.

"You're about my size," McGrady commented, studying Bob Lewis's thick build. "I'll need a ranger's jacket and hat. And one of those clipboards you carry around."

"Sure thing."

"Is there some place where Officer Rogers can view the camper without being seen?"

"Sure. The laundry and shower building. He can go in the back way, and find a position at one of the front windows. The camper in question is parked in a site a little north." He pointed out the window. "You can see the roof of the laundry building through those trees."

McGrady nodded at Rogers. "Keep a lookout from there. We'll approach the camper as if we're making some kind of a ranger check. If there's any kind of trouble, radio for a backup unit."

"Yes, sir." The plainclothes officer quickly left the station and disappeared through the trees in the direction of the laundry building.

Neil wished he could change into ranger's clothes and join the surveillance, but he knew better than to argue with McGrady. If word came back that it was Billie Mae, Courtney would need him to be with her. Both McGrady and the ranger wore gun holsters under their jackets, and probably considered his unarmed presence a risk.

When Courtney saw the guns, she paled. The woman had a gun, and she'd killed before. In a showdown with police, would she sacrifice the baby to save her own miserable skin?

"There's coffee in the kitchen," the ranger offered, as if trying to ease the tense situation. Neither Neil nor Courtney responded even though neither of them had eaten lunch.

As McGrady and the ranger left the station, Courtney and Neil watched through the front window. Since the station was built at a slightly higher elevation than the rest of the campground, they could glimpse cars, trailers, campers and campsites along a narrow road snaking through stands of pine, cedar and aspen trees.

McGrady and the ranger walked down the gravel road at a seemingly leisurely pace. Courtney swallowed hard as she watched.

Hurry! Hurry! The word was a drum beating in her head. When McGrady and the ranger disappeared from sight, she turned away from the window. She hugged herself as if she were about to break apart, and began pacing up and down. Adrenaline fired every cell in her body, demanding release.

"Easy does it," Neil cautioned, fighting his own battle to remain calm as he ran agitated fingers through his hair.

A large round clock on the wall ticked off the excruciating minutes. As they waited, they kept glancing out the front window. It seemed as if an hour had passed, but in reality, it was less than ten minutes when Officer Rogers came into sight. He ran toward the station with his two-way radio pressed to his ear.

Courtney and Neil bounded out of the station and met him on the front steps. They both talked at once, bombarding him.

"What happened?"

"Was it her?"

"My baby?"

He shook his head. "The camper was empty even before I took up my position. Looks hastily abandoned. We've called in backup units. McGrady wants you to come and see if you can identify any of the baby stuff."

Baby stuff!

Neil grabbed her hand as they ran down the road.

Shaded by huge ponderosa pines and set back from the road, the campsite would have been inconspicuous under normal circumstances, but Courtney's chest nearly exploded when they reached it.

McGrady stood in the doorway of a small snub-nosed camper, parked in campsite number twenty-nine. Ranger Lewis was outside, his eyes searching the ground as he circled the camper and made his way through wild grass and mountain shrubs.

McGrady motioned them inside. "Take a look, Courtney, and see if anything looks familiar."

The clutter was unbelievable. Boxes, dirty dishes, cans of food, baby paraphernalia and clothes were strewn from one end to the other. Every square inch of the small camper had been utilized to provide a miniature galley, a combination couch-bed, one small table for eating and a postage-stamp-size bathroom.

Courtney's eyes passed over it all with driving urgency. Breakfast was still on the table, and there were signs of a hasty departure.

"The ranger's attention this morning must have alerted her," Neil said, his chest tightening.

McGrady nodded. "She left in a hurry, all right."

"We've still got to verify that Jamie is the baby she has with her," McGrady reminded them.

Courtney knew they were looking to her for that confirmation. There was plenty of evidence of a baby in the small camper, but none of the stuff was familiar. All of Jamie's used belongings had been left in the houseboat. The only thing she was sure had been taken was Jamie's carrier, and there was no sign of it in the camper.

"How about this toy?"

"This bottle?"

Neil and McGrady kept showing her all the baby stuff they could find. She shook her head.

None of it had been Jamie's. Courtney was about to despair when they moved a pile of bedding on the couch and she glimpsed the corner of a familiar blanket.

She grabbed it as if she'd found a treasure. "It's Jamie's." With tears in her eyes, she pressed the soft flannel against her face.

"Are you sure?" Neil questioned. One baby blanket looked like any other to him.

"Positive. I made it for him. See the edging? One of my feeble attempts at crocheting."

It was Neil who found the footlocker. "I'll be damned, would you look at this."

"What is it?" the detective asked.

"Take a look."

McGrady's expression matched Neil's as he stared at the gray wig, mustache, cowboy hat, an empty gun holster and a couple of loose bullets.

"Your bank robber," Neil said evenly. "What's this?" He lifted out a photo of a rough, hard-looking man with piercing black eyes.

"Buzzy Kline, if I'm not mistaken. Killed in a bank robbery a while back. Billie's accomplice."

Courtney's eyes went first to the empty gun holster. She paled. "She's armed."

If they cornered the woman, and she shot her way out, what would happen to Jamie?

Courtney's reaction was one of instant anger.

"Why did you let her get away!" she lashed out at McGrady. "She was here this morning, the ranger said so. She had my baby, and—"

Neil touched her arm. "Easy, honey."

She shook off his hand and continued to blast McGrady. "You waited too long. Why didn't you do something when the ranger called you?"

"I did," he answered in a calm tone that was a sharp contrast to her verbal attack. "I immediately closed off the roads. There's no way she could have driven away after that."

"Then where is she?"

"Somewhere in the park."

His calm answer only infuriated her further. "How many hundred acres is that?"

He ignored the question. "Now that I have verification that she's the kidnapper of your baby, I'll call in as much manpower as we need. In the meantime, you two stay here." He gave Neil his cell phone number. "If you see anything, call."

Neil knew it would take time to organize a search party. At least an hour or more. The anger and frustration surging through his body needed some release. He was just as capable of joining the search as anyone, but something in the detective's steady eyes warned him not to argue.

As McGrady started toward the door, Ranger Lewis appeared.

"I checked the perimeter," he told the detective. "Looks like someone hurriedly made their way through the area in back of the camper. There're broken twigs and footprints in the deadfall. The size could be a woman's but the prints seem too heavily pressed into the dirt for normal weight."

"She could have been weighed down by the baby, especially if she had him in a carrier," McGrady replied.

"Two trails are only a short distance away. One leads down to a small camping area beside a stream, and the other doubles back toward the main road. We'll have to send search parties in both directions."

"Let's get on it." McGrady started out the door with the ranger.

"I'm coming, too." Courtney was ready to bolt after them.

"The woman's got a gun." Neil grabbed her. "Nothing would please her more than to use it on

you. Getting yourself shot isn't going to help anyone."

"It's my baby!" Courtney protested. "Why can't
I be out there looking like anyone else?"

"Because you're too emotionally involved, and
you don't know the area. Tracking someone in these
mountains takes skill and training. McGrady doesn't
want to put you in harm's way." Neil gathered her
close. "And neither do I."

"Maybe she'll run back here." Courtney stiffened
at the thought. "I wish she would."

Neil hadn't considered that possibility. A cold
prickling rose on his neck. If she burst into the
camper, gun in hand, they'd be like sitting ducks.

Courtney couldn't sit still. She gathered up all the
baby clothes, toys and diapers, and packed them in
one of the suitcases. As all of "Devanna's" shopping
trips came back to haunt her, she was relieved that
Jamie hadn't wanted for anything while he was in the
woman's clutches.

"Good idea." Neil was relieved she was putting
some of that nervous energy to good use. When she
examined the refrigerator and found two baby bottles of prepared formula, her face went white. Had
Billie left in too much of a hurry to take them with
her? What would she do when it was time to feed
him? It was already time for his afternoon bottle.

She began frantically looking for the diaper bag.

"What is it?" Neil asked, seeing her frantic search.

As Courtney drew out a brown leather bag from
under the daybed, she wailed, "She left without it.
No bottles, no diapers."

"Maybe she packed them in something else," he soothed, as he sat down beside her and let her bury her head against his chest.

The wait was even more excruciating than the one at the ranger station. When they heard someone coming up to the door, they both froze.

"Hello." A timid knock echoed the greeting.

Neil pushed Courtney behind him as he went to the door. A small, bald-headed man holding a small box of laundry soap looked at Neil questioningly.

"Is the lady here?"

"No," Neil answered evenly.

"Well, she loaned my wife a cup of soap the other day when they were doing laundry, and we wanted to pay it back." He handed Neil the box. "Tell her, thank you."

"I will," Neil assured him. "You haven't seen her this morning, have you? My wife and I paid her a surprise visit, but she doesn't seem to be around."

"No, we left early this morning on a sunrise hike. Just got back. Sorry. Maybe if you ask around?"

"Yes, maybe we'll do that."

After the man had left, Neil looked at Courtney, thoughtfully.

They weren't equipped to join any search party, but there were some things they could do. Sitting around, waiting for something to happen was driving him nuts. "What do you think?" he asked Courtney.

"About what?"

"We could walk through the campground. Talk to people. Maybe turn up something that might help.

She's bound to have made contact with some other people, like that guy's wife."

Courtney's face brightened. "Yes, we can do that. McGrady will probably be pleased."

Neil wasn't so sure, but he couldn't see what they had to lose.

He took her arm. "Let's go."

After all, what harm could come from chatting with a bunch of friendly campers?

Chapter Fifteen

Courtney and Neil looked for signs that McGrady's organized search parties had arrived, but the campground seemed as peaceful as ever.

"They're probably concentrating on securing the areas around the campground," Neil speculated. "Like casting a net, they'll tighten the perimeter, and men and dogs will move in until they find her."

"Someone is bound to have seen her leave," Courtney insisted. "There are kids and adults all over the place. A woman carrying a baby carrier would stand out. All we have to do is ask around."

Courtney's hopeful expectations soon proved to be ill-founded as they went from one camping site to the next asking adults and children alike if they'd seen a middle-aged woman with a baby that morning.

Even families occupying the sites closest to Billie's camper shook their heads and admitted they weren't even aware that a lone woman was the occupant.

The responses were varied, but equally discouraging.

"Sorry, we just pulled in last night."

"Nope, I got up at dawn to go fishing."

"There are women and babies all over the place," one man retorted. "What's special about this one?"

Neil put a firm hand on Courtney's arm before she could answer. If the news of an armed kidnapper spread through the campground, the whole camping community might panic. Well-meaning sympathizers could just muddy the waters with half-truths in an effort to help.

Frustrated and disappointed, Courtney fought back angry tears as they came up with absolutely nothing at the end of their canvass of the camping sites in the immediate area where the camper had been parked.

"I think we ought to check the bait shop and laundry room," Neil said, still hopeful they would run into someone who had seen Billie that morning. He knew that fishermen came and went on the paths that led down to the stream. If Billie fled that way, one of them might have seen her.

"I'll get the laundry," Courtney said, and headed in that direction. Keeping up with the baby's washing would cause Billie to make frequent trips to the laundry room, and apparently she'd been pleasant enough to loan another woman some soap.

"Yeah, I remember her," a young woman attendant in charge said in response to Courtney's description. "She was kind of a funny duck."

"Why do you say that?"

"I saw her washing a lot of baby stuff, and I thought she must be a grandma. Just trying to be friendly, and make conversation, I asked her about the baby. Wow, what a mistake. She looked at me, all daggers, and stomped out of here." She shook her head. "Go figure that one."

"How about this morning?"

"Yep, she was here early."

"We're trying to find out where she might have gone after she left here. Did you see her later on anywhere?"

She shook her head. "You might ask Ranger Lewis. I saw him talking to her."

Courtney repeated the conversation to Neil when he returned empty-handed from his visit to the bait house. The attendant's information just verified Ranger Lewis's reported contact.

"Maybe if he hadn't said anything to her, she wouldn't have taken the baby and fled," Courtney lamented.

"She hadn't planned on leaving, that's obvious from the condition of the camper," Neil agreed. "Maybe it was her encounter with the ranger, or something else. In any case, I think we should keep asking around."

They had covered the main area of the campground, but Neil knew that there were other sites along two narrow roads running in opposite directions from the center campground.

"Why don't we split up? That way we can cover more campsites faster." An urgency had been mounting inside Courtney with every fruitless minute.

"I have a better suggestion. Why don't you wait at the station, and let me do the footwork."

An icy cold glare was his answer. "If we learn anything important, we can head back to the ranger station and contact McGrady right away."

"Okay, but we'll meet here first. You wait if I'm not back when you get here."

Courtney nodded in agreement and headed in one direction while Neil went in another. As before, they each stopped at every site, asking their well-worn question, and getting the same negative results.

Neil stopped to talk to families collected around picnic tables and barbecue grills, but came up empty without any helpful information.

He stopped several hikers returning to the campground, hoping they might have spied a woman and a baby somewhere along the trail.

"Nope. Sorry."

He boldly knocked on an assortment of recreational vehicles, and got the same negative answers as he did from people who were camping out in tents.

When he met a couple of young boys who had been fishing in a nearby stream, he asked them if they'd seen a woman with a baby.

"Nope," the oldest boy replied. "But we saw plenty of trout jumping around, didn't we, Luke? Lookee." He opened the fishing basket to show Neil their catch.

The contrast between their high spirits and his own leaden feelings only heightened his growing frustration.

Activity was everywhere. Children bounded around, squealing. Tethered dogs wagged their tails and yapped to get attention. Adults sat in lawn chairs, laughing and joking as they sipped drinks.

As he passed a luxurious RV, the total absence of any activity caught his attention. No sign of life inside or outside. On such a warm day, you'd think the door or windows would be open to catch the cool mountain breeze, he thought as he made his way to the door.

His knock echoed in the total silence. Nobody home. Maybe they were hikers or fishermen like the boys. He wondered if McGrady's men were checking the lakes and streams, or just concentrating on the wooded areas.

He started to turn away when a faint sound stopped him. Even before he fully recognized it as a baby's cry, the door flew open, and the gun in Billie Mae Kessel's steady hand was pointed at his head.

His heart stopped. His last breath burned in his lungs. Never in the world had he expected to find her himself. The most he had hoped for was to find someone who might have seen her leave the campground.

Now he knew the truth. *She'd never left!* A crazed glint in her eyes warned him not to make any sudden moves.

"Get in here before I blow your brains out." Her finger trembled on the trigger as she motioned him inside.

One section of the RV had been expanded and the spacious sitting area was almost as large as a mobile home, and as beautifully furnished.

A fussy Jamie was lying on a daybed. His pacifier had dropped out of his mouth, and he was kicking and waving his arms in protest.

A white-faced, gray-haired couple huddled together in a sitting position on the carpeted floor. Their frightened eyes pleaded with Neil to do something.

"She's going to kill us," the woman wailed. Her whole body shivered with fear, and her terrified, white-lipped husband looked ready to have a heart attack.

"Shut your trap!" Billie ordered. "One more peep out of you, and you'll get it now instead of later. You're only alive because I need you to drive this thing out of the park when it gets dark."

"Down!" Billie motioned Neil to the floor, and her eyes glinted with a strange kind of power. "You're not so high and mighty now, are you?" A low rumble of satisfied laughter came deep from her chest, but there was no mirth in it, only hatred.

Neil's skin crawled as he realized how twisted her mind was. How could he appeal to any decent behavior when the term had no meaning for her?

"You thought I was dirt under your feet, didn't you? Flashing around in your boat and fancy car. I told Buzz all about you. He damn well knows how to handle the likes of you."

"Buzz?" Neil echoed. He searched his memory. Wasn't that the name of her partner who had been killed in an aborted robbery? Buzzy Kline. Why was she speaking about him in the present tense?

"Yes, Buzz. He's my man," she answered, defiantly. "And he's taking good care of me and Jesse."

"Jesse?"

"Our baby. That's what we named him." She smiled in a secret kind of way as she sat down on the daybed beside Jamie. Keeping her gun leveled at her prisoners, she gave him back the pacifier.

"It's a nice name," Neil responded as evenly as he could. If he could get her distracted by talking, she might get careless. "How did you decide on Jesse?"

"Buzz's grandpa was named Jesse," she mused as she stroked the baby's soft head with her free hand. "I didn't like it real well, but when Buzz insisted, I finally said, okay. You don't argue with Buzz when he sets his mind." Her eyelids flickered as if she remembered a time when she'd learned that lesson.

"He sounds like a smart man," Neil said, as his mind raced to find a way to use the woman's fixation on her dead partner. He knew if the demented woman lost it, she might begin shooting. Thank God Courtney wasn't with him. Billie might have shot her on sight.

"Damn right, Buzz is smart. We hit a dozen banks. Got away scot-free every time." She laughed again. "We had them cops going in every direction. Left a few of them lying in the dust, too."

He took a quick breath to steady his voice. "Buzz wouldn't want Ja—Jesse to get hurt, would he?"

Neil knew he'd said the wrong thing when her expression changed and her whole body stiffened. She frowned and nodded as if listening to instructions from someone.

Neil's worst fears were realized when she stood up, centering a hard, unwavering gaze on him. "Buzz says you're inching for a bullet between your eyes."

"No, Billie, no. Don't do it. Someone will hear the shots," Neil quickly warned her.

She hesitated as Jamie began to cry, getting louder and louder with every breath. As she stood there, her gun poised to fire, she seemed torn between the baby's care and her need to carry out Buzz's orders.

"Someone will hear him crying," Neil warned.

"Shut up!"

"He's probably hungry or needs his diaper changed. Courtney said you always took good care of Ja—Jesse."

The cold indifference that had been on her face was slowly replaced by a faint acknowledgment of his compliment. "Better than she did. A lot better. Jesse knows it, too."

The baby was thrusting his arms and legs in every direction. His wails were getting louder and louder. Neil saw Billie glance at a pocket in the carrier lying a few feet away. An empty bottle stuck out of one pocket. In her haste she must have only brought one bottle, he thought. Courtney had found the others in the refrigerator.

Billie sat down beside the crying baby, but there was little she could do to placate him, and still keep a gun on her hostages.

"Why don't I heat a bottle for him, and change his diaper?"

"I don't have any more."

"I bet these folks have some milk in the fridge that I could heat up," Neil offered, playing for time.

"He has to have formula," Billie repeated firmly as if she'd heard Courtney instructing her.

"Oh, Ja—Jesse's a big boy now. A bottle of real milk won't hurt him. He's not going to settle down until he's fed and changed," Neil said firmly. "Someone's going to hear him."

As if his words were magic, the door vibrated with a loud knocking. Even as he prayed it wouldn't be, when Billie jerked open the door, Courtney stood there. If Billie's gun hadn't been pointed at her heart, Neil would have jumped Billie from behind, but he couldn't take a chance of the gun going off.

Courtney's startled eyes didn't focus on Billie or the gun, but on her baby. Neil doubted if Courtney even heard the flow of swear words as Billie motioned her inside and ordered her down on the floor a good distance from Neil and the other two hostages.

"Do as she says," Neil warned Courtney. He was afraid if she ran over to Jamie, Billie might shoot her before she reached him. "The baby's hungry. She's going to let me fix him a bottle, aren't you, Billie?"

"Any funny business, and I'll kill the lot of you. Got it?" she demanded, keeping the gun on Courtney.

"I got it." He rose slowly to his feet. "I'll wash the empty bottle, heat the milk, and change Jesse's diaper. My sister has a baby the same age," he added, in hopes that it would reassure her he knew what he was doing.

She turned the gun in his direction as he took the empty bottle out of the carrier's pocket, and found one diaper left in the bottom.

"Be damn quick about it," Billie ordered as the baby continued to cry.

He sent a silent warning to Courtney as he crossed the floor within inches of where she was sitting.

"I could help," the older woman spoke up to everyone's surprise. She'd stopped her cowering sniffles, and her husband put a warning hand on her shoulder.

Billie's face flushed with fury as she pointed the gun at her. "Shut up! One more peep out of you, and it'll be your last. I'm running the show here, and don't you forget it."

The kitchen was at the far end of the RV, just outside a door leading into the bedroom. Neil was in plain view of the sitting area as he moved about. He found a half quart of milk in the refrigerator and decided against taking time to sterilize the bottle and nipple, trusting that the steamy hot water would suffice.

Courtney kept her eyes glued on her infant son. The torture of sitting just a few feet from him was beyond belief. How could she cower on the floor when her baby was crying and needing attention? Every motherly instinct threatened her self-control.

Billie sat down beside Jamie, and for the moment, the baby accepted his pacifier again. Staring at Courtney, the woman frowned and seemed to be listening to that inner voice. Several times, she nodded, and once even laughed and said something under her breath.

Goose bumps prickled on Courtney's neck. Now she knew. There hadn't been any radio in her room! This crazed woman had been laughing and talking to herself into the night. Courtney shuddered as a flood of memories came back to haunt her, and the present moment seemed totally unreal.

She'd waited for Neil to meet her as arranged, and when he didn't show, she'd started walking in his direction, expecting to meet him. When she neared the end of the camping site, she ran into a couple of kids sitting on a log, eating lunch.

When she described Neil and asked if they'd seen him, one of the boys nodded. "I saw him go in there a little while ago."

He pointed at a luxurious RV a few campsites away. Even before she'd reached the door, she heard a baby crying.

Now she feasted on the sight of Jamie like a starving person lusting for food. She ached to pick him up and hold him close, but fear of the woman sitting beside him kept her motionless. Her baby was alive and well, she kept telling herself. For the moment that had to be enough.

As her eyes shifted to the older couple huddled on the floor, her heart sickened. She realized Billie had four hostages in her power, and would callously use every one of them to her advantage.

By the time Neil returned with the full bottle and the diaper, Jamie had spit out his pacifier and was starting to cry again.

"Do you want to feed and change him?" Neil asked, offering them to Billie.

For a second Billie's eyes flickered in indecision. Then she smiled as if she realized he'd been trying to trick her.

"How stupid do you think I am?" She leveled the

gun at him as she stood up and motioned for him to take her place on the daybed.

As he replaced the baby's wet diaper with a dry one, his mind raced to find a way to get the firearm from her. No telling what the voice in her head was saying. At any moment, she could turn the gun on Courtney and finish what she'd failed three times to do. Time was running out. He had to do something before it was too late. The baby was the main thing she cared about. The baby was her Achilles' heel, and he decided on a desperate move.

He finished fastening the diaper and then lurched to his feet. Holding the baby out in front of him, he faced Billie. "Here catch!"

As he feigned to throw the baby at her, she shrieked, dropped the gun and prepared to catch the baby.

Neil moved quickly, kicking the gun over to Courtney, and then backing up with Jamie out of Billie's reach.

Courtney grabbed up the army revolver, and held it with both hands as she got to her feet. Her hands were surprisingly steady and her expression purposeful as she pointed it at the woman who had murdered two innocent people and put her through hell.

The rage she had felt so many times swelled up within her. Her finger trembled on the trigger, and in that frozen moment, it was her baby's cry that jerked her back from the edge of revenge.

"Take Jamie in the bedroom and feed him," Neil ordered as he carefully took the gun and handed her the baby.

Billie seemed totally confused. She started to follow Courtney. Neil stepped in front of her and buried the end of the gun in her stomach.

"Give me one reason not to blow your guts out."

"Buzz will take care of you," she snarled like a cornered cat as she backed up. The wild look in her eyes sickened Neil.

"I got some rope to tie her up," the older man said with renewed spirit as he helped his wife to her feet.

"Good, get it."

They forced Billie to sit down in the passenger's seat of the RV and tied her firmly in it. Then Neil took out his cell phone and dialed the number Mc-Grady had given him.

When the detective answered, Neil said simply, "We got her."

"What?"

"We've got Billie Mae Kessel. She's tied up, ready for delivery."

Neil wished he could have seen McGrady's face when he heard the story of her capture. There was relief and disbelief in his quick response. "We'll be there in a few minutes. Can you keep things under control until then?"

"We'll try, sir," Neil responded solemnly. A broad smile crossed his lips as he hung up. He turned to the owners of the RV. "Are you folks all right?"

"We are now," the man responded. "I'm Ned Waits, and this is my wife, Alice. We're mighty grateful you took care of her the way you did."

"We thought we were goners," his wife admitted.

"Try to relax, if you can. Police officers will be here shortly," Neil told them.

"I'd better make some coffee," Alice said as she visibly straightened up and squared her shoulders.

Neil smiled, recognizing she came from the old school, like his mother, who met every crisis with food and drink. "You keep an eye on our prisoner," she told her husband, knowing he needed to be kept busy, as well.

Neil hurried into the bedroom to make sure Courtney and the baby were all right. She was lying on the bed with the sleeping baby in the crook of her arm. As she smiled up at him with an expression of total happiness, he thought she was the most beautiful woman he had ever seen.

They just looked at each other as love radiated between them. Then he lay down on the bed, facing her, with the baby between them.

Smiling tenderly at her, he whispered, "We ought to do this more often."

"Yes," she whispered gratefully.

"Like forever?"

"Forever and ever."

When he leaned over and kissed her, she knew that somehow, in the midst of a terrifying ordeal, they had become a family.

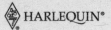

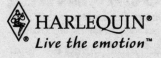

If you enjoyed what you just read,
then we've got an offer you can't resist!

Take 2 bestselling love stories FREE!

Plus get a FREE surprise gift!

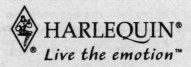

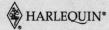

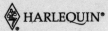